Katherine Shonk

THE RED PASSPORT

A BEGUILING DEBUT COLLECTION SET IN THE "NEW RUSSIA" ABOUT LOVE, DISLOCATION, AND THE STRUGGLE TO GET A FOOTHOLD IN A CHANGING WORLD

The unpredictable, poignant, and often comic stories that make up Katherine Shonk's *The Red Passport* portray the tumult, hopes, and disappointments of Russians and foreigners alike in post-Communist Russia. Many of the Russians in these stories are strangers in their own country, learning to navigate a new landscape of Dunkin' Donuts franchises that flourish where consumer culture had so recently been anathema; where the fall of the Soviet Union has not brought about peace or prosperity; and where people still find a way to reach out for love, despite often disastrous results. "My Mother's Garden" is a parable of broken promises—an old woman living near Chernobyl does not understand why she can't eat those lovely, robust onions, better than any she'd grown for decades. "Our American" tells the story of a thirteen-year-old boy who watches with fascination and dread as his older brother, a veteran of the Chechen war, pursues the American girl next door. "The Young People of Moscow" describes an extraordinary day in the life of an aging couple selling Soviet poetry in an underground bazaar. In her crystalline stories, Shonk finds both the nub of her characters' disappointment and the truth of their good intentions. Describing a place that is at once exotic and disconcertingly familiar, *The Red Passport* is a moving and startling book that doles out amazement and delight in equal measure.

KATHERINE SHONK was born in Chicago and lives in Evanston, Illinois. Her stories have appeared in *Tin House*, *Story Quarterly*, and *American Short Fiction* and have been reprinted in *Best American Short Stories*.

5 1/2 x 8 1/4 / 224 pages
0-374-24847-8
$22.00/$36.50 CANADIAN

THE RED PASSPORT

THE RED PASSPORT

KATHERINE SHONK

FARRAR · STRAUS · GIROUX / NEW YORK

Farrar, Straus and Giroux
19 Union Square West, New York 10003

Library of Congress Cataloging-in-Publication Data TK

"My Mother's Garden" appeared, in slightly different form, in *Tin House* and *Best American Short Stories 2001*. "The Young People of Moscow" appeared, in slightly different form, in *StoryQuarterly* with the title "Children's Verse". "The Death of Olga Vasilievna" appeared, in slightly different form, in *American Short Fiction*.

Grateful acknowledgment is made to Actes Sud for their kind permission to reproduce excerpts from *C'est moi qi souligne* by Nina Berberova, copyright © 1989, Actes Sud.

Design by Jonathan D. Lippincott

www.fsgbooks.com

1   3   5   7   9   10   8   6   4   2

FOR MY FAMILY

CONTENTS

THE RED PASSPORT

THE DEATH OF
OLGA VASILIEVNA

Andrei was returning with his wife, Sveta, from her mother's burial in a cemetery in southwest Moscow when he spotted a young woman displaying a basket of kittens in the middle of Revolution Square metro station. "Look," he said, steering Sveta around a statue of an alert soldier, his pistol worn by passersby to a thin golden pipe. The woman, who wore a fox-fur coat and had a cigarette hanging from her mouth, held the basket out to them.

"Oh, how sweet!" Sveta said.

Amid the gray and white squirming balls, a kitten darker and smaller than the rest sat as still and black as the forged revolutionaries who crouched beneath the station's wide arches. The kitten had a white spot on its neck. Its eyes were fixed on Sveta.

"This little boy likes you," Andrei said, scooping it up.

"What makes you think it's a boy?" Sveta scratched the kitten behind the ears. Her weariness was gone, her face rosy and untroubled above her black coat and mourning dress.

Andrei shrugged. He had imagined that when they finally got a cat, it would be a boy. Sveta had begged for a cat for years, but her mother, Olga Vasilievna, had forbidden it. The woman had died of a heart attack in her sleep four days ago. Andrei flipped the kitten over, allowing Sveta to poke under its stubby tail. The animal gazed at Andrei serenely from its up-side-down position.

"*Koshka,*" Sveta said with satisfaction. It was a girl, after all. "How much?"

"Thirty thousand," the young woman said.

"Thirty thousand!"

The woman claimed the cats' mother was a Persian and pulled a scrap of paper from her coat pocket as proof. Sveta frowned at the smudged certificate, then counted twenty-seven thousand rubles into the woman's hand. Both women looked at Andrei; he added a metro token to the pile. The woman grimaced and shooed them off.

The cat perched on Sveta's shoulder, peering at Andrei and its surroundings with calm curiosity as they took the subway seven stops, chugged up the long escalator into the cool February sun, pushed into the crowded bus that delivered them to their zone of apartments, and rode the creaking elevator to the tenth floor.

Andrei and Sveta set a fine celebratory table: a bottle of Sovietskoye champagne, a tin of sprats, cheese and bread, and, for dessert, a chocolate cake imported from Denmark. It was a light meal, vaguely exotic, unlike anything Olga Vasilievna had ever served, and funded by money Sveta had taken from her mother's wallet that morning before the funeral. Soon the only sounds in the apartment were the soft smacking of the kitten's mouth—they had fed her kasha doused with juice from the sprats—and the tinkling of Sveta's and Andrei's spoons as they dissolved sugar in their glasses of dry champagne.

"Our first night alone," Sveta said.

"M-hmm."

"This is our place now."

"Yes. Our own home, for the first time."

Sveta reached for Andrei's hand across the table. "I've waited three years to be alone with you."

"As have I." In truth, Andrei had rarely considered what life would be like without Olga Vasilievna; he was surprised by how much her sudden passing moved him. He and Sveta had spent the past several evenings visiting with the dead woman's relatives, drinking and reminiscing. It was remarkable to Andrei how few mourners his mother-in-law had and how easily distracted they were from their grief.

"Andrei?" Sveta rubbed his knuckle.

"Yes?"

"Andrei, I've been a child until now, living in my mother's house, bickering with her all the time." Letting go of his hand, she lifted her long auburn hair and twisted it behind her head. "But now it's time to accept adult responsibilities."

Andrei raised his glass. "To responsibility."

"Because tonight we are adults." They clinked glasses and sipped. "Besides, we have a little one to look after now." She nodded at the kitten. "What should we name her?"

"Pavlov," Andrei said. "Because I'll train her according to proven scientific methods." Last year they had taken Sveta's niece to Moscow's cat circus, where house cats raced across high wires and jumped through hoops to get to the kibble concealed in the clowns' fists. Before that day, Andrei had not shared Sveta's desire for a cat, but at the circus he was struck by the idea that with proper motivation, even such independent spirits would respond predictably to human whims.

"Well, she's a girl, so she can be Pavlova. A cat with intelligence *and* grace."

"Just like her mother," he said, getting up to kiss her.

That night they made love for the first time since Olga Vasilievna's death. Sveta floated silently above Andrei in the dark. Had she cried out in the past merely from a desire to aggravate her mother? The kitten stared at them, unblinking, from the floor. Afterward, she settled in the crook of Sveta's neck, and Andrei watched them both drift into sleep.

He remembered the last time Sveta raised the subject of getting a cat, just a few weeks ago. Olga Vasilievna had been frying chicken legs, scraping the cast-iron pan back and forth across the burner. "Don't I have enough mouths to feed?" the old woman said, and glanced at Andrei, who was strumming minor chords on his guitar at the kitchen table.

"I've wanted a cat my whole life," Sveta said. "I'm twenty-three years old." She was slicing an apple with a paring knife made razor sharp from Andrei's patient honing, its wooden handle worn to a petrified stub. "How long do I have to wait?"

"You'll get your cat when I'm in the ground." Olga Vasilievna's broad face was damp and flushed. "You'll get your cat, and then you'll be sorry. Will your cat buy fresh bread for you every day? Will your cat bring in a pension?"

"When this apartment is ours, I won't miss your pathetic pension." Tossing the knife in the sink, Sveta stalked out of the room and slammed the bedroom door behind her.

"You'll be stuck here with a hungry cat and a lazy husband, and you'll remember how easy you had it! Svetlana!" Olga Vasilievna turned to look at Andrei, whose fingers had frozen on the guitar strings.

Andrei and his co-workers at the chemical research laboratory had stopped receiving their salaries the previous summer. By November, Andrei's friend Dima had convinced him that they should quit their jobs as lab assistants and launch careers as travel agents. Andrei could not picture himself behind a desk, selling tours to Cyprus or the Seychelles, but he was persuaded by Dima's assurances of a high salary and free vacations.

On Andrei and Dima's last day of work, the scientists cleared test tubes and microscopes from a black lab table to make way for bottles of vodka and cognac. Andrei's supervisor caught his eye across the smoke and candlelight. "What a sad boy, our Andryusha," Lushin said. "Such tragic eyes, like a poet. He looks like Brodsky." They toasted Brodsky, who had died the week before, across the ocean in New York. Lushin splashed their glasses with another round of cognac. "And to Andrei, the next Brodsky!"

They all laughed, but later, as Andrei stumbled home, the toast echoed in his head. He repeated it to Sveta that night in bed. "Lushin saw into my soul. He saw that I want to be a poet."

"Why didn't you tell me?" Sveta said, holding him in her arms.

Andrei didn't answer. In fact, it had never occurred to him to write poetry for a living, or to write poetry at all—which made the discovery all the more mysterious and urgent.

"While you're looking for a new job, you'll have time to write," Sveta added.

How wonderful to have a wife who understands me, Andrei thought sleepily.

And so he put off joining Dima in his search for a job as a travel agent and instead, during the hour Sveta and her mother watched *Santa Barbara*, locked himself in the bathroom and sat in the empty bathtub with a notebook and pencil. Over the past three months Andrei had filled many pages with doodles and drawings of his feet, but he had not yet written a poem, or even a line or phrase that might one day become a poem. Still, he felt certain that if he continued his routine, inspiration would eventually strike.

The household survived without his income up until Olga Vasilievna's death. Sveta's brother took care of their mother's funeral expenses, and the dead woman's final pension payment had been finished off on dinner and a cat.

The next morning, when Andrei awoke, Pavlova was pressed against his neck and Sveta was sitting on the floor in a pool of sunlight, poring over the English-language newspaper. Several days later she was called in to interview with an American accounting firm for a position as a secretary. Sveta had graduated from a business institute the previous year with a specialization in English and computers, but since then she had continued to sell shoes part-time in a kiosk under the Garden Ring Road.

"I should wear a suit, a very smart suit, but this will have to do," she said, plucking stray cat hairs from her old green sweater and the brown skirt she had sewn herself. She held out her hand for Andrei to shake. "I am very pleased to meet you," she said in English. "I know many computer programs. I am a hard worker. I look forward to hearing from you."

Sveta left, and Andrei lay down on the bed with his notebook. He balled up one of his foot drawings and tossed it across the room. As if she'd been waiting for him to begin her training, the kitten sprang from beneath the bed and snatched the ball in her teeth, then trotted back to Andrei and dropped it in front of him. Andrei threw the ball again and again until Pavlova, panting like a dog, collapsed against his chest.

They awoke to the sound of a key in the door. The sun had disappeared behind the white apartment block that mirrored theirs.

"Andreiiiii!" Sveta threw herself on top of him; the cat skittered across the room. "Feel how fast my heart's beating." She pressed Andrei's hand to the hollow of her chest. "Andrei, they're going to pay me six hundred dollars a month!"

Andrei reached for his cigarettes. Their monthly household income—Andrei's former salary, Olga Vasilievna's pension, and Sveta's earnings from the shoe kiosk—had been small enough to count in rubles. "It is good," he said in English. "You are the good girl."

"I am *a* good girl." Sveta sat up and held his hands. "Now, Andrei. There is no need for you to work right now. You can stay at home and write poetry. I'll support you."

He smiled. He was sorry he had told Sveta of his dream of

becoming a poet. "I'm not an artist. I haven't written anything
. . . good."

"You will," Sveta said. "You'll become a famous poet, and
you'll be invited to read your poetry in Europe and America,
and we'll travel the world."

"Now you're making fun of me."

"Andrei." She locked his gaze with hers. "You told me you
wanted to be a great writer. Are you going to try, or aren't
you?"

He looked into Sveta's eyes and imagined himself seeking
out her face as he read poetry in crowded auditoriums in St.
Petersburg and New York City. "It won't happen overnight,"
he said.

"What filth," he wrote that evening in the bathtub. "What
filth, your gulf fish." Nonsense from a popular movie that aired
every New Year's Eve. Quietly, he tore the page into thin strips
and flushed them down the toilet.

Andrei could not recall being bored before Olga Vasilievna
died, before Sveta started her new job. Even after he quit
working at the lab, there had always been something to do—
search the hardware marketplace for washers and nails, silently
pass the newspaper puzzle back and forth with his mother-in-
law, sit in Sveta's kiosk breathing in the smell of shoe leather.
But with both of them gone, there was nothing to do but sleep,
strum his guitar, and play with the cat. Pavlova was growing
into an adolescent, coltish and lean. Andrei developed a
method of waving his foot that kept her balanced on her hind
legs, at first for just a second or two, then five or six, until he
finally relented and gave her a scrap of cheese.

Every evening Sveta returned home chattering about life at
the accounting office. She was personal secretary to an American manager named Melissa, who happened to be married to

one of the firm's partners, which gave Sveta's position added prestige. Melissa had just had a baby, and twice a day she would close the door of her office and later emerge with a bottle of fresh breast milk acquired with the aid of a small electric-powered pump. Sveta was responsible for taking the bottle to one of the firm's drivers, who would promptly deliver it to the baby's nanny.

One night, Sveta opened an envelope and silently fanned six hundred-dollar bills on the kitchen table. Benjamin Franklin was as fat and stern as the ringmaster of the cat circus. Andrei turned from the disapproving scowls and, spotting the cat, kicked off a slipper and wiggled his foot. "Svet, look." Pavlova wobbled about on her hind legs, her mouth open in pursuit.

"The ballerina dances." Sveta stood up to refresh the teapot with hot water. "Andrei?"

The cat crouched, tail wagging. Andrei had forgotten the cheese.

"How's your writing going?" she asked.

"Not bad." Andrei still locked himself in the bathtub when Sveta turned on *Santa Barbara*, but the routine had begun to feel more like a sentence than a retreat.

"Maybe one day you'll share some of your poems with me."

Pavlova lunged. Andrei winced as a claw pricked his toe.

Andrei sat in the lobby of the travel agency, sipping the warm cola the receptionist had given him and watching a video advertising the firm's package vacations to Egypt. In a glass-walled office to his right, Dima was talking to a young couple. He signaled Andrei with a nod.

As Andrei watched the video, he imagined heading off to the desert, leaving Sveta lying by the hotel pool in a bikini. Surely the pyramids would inspire him, and he would read his poems to her on the balcony in the late afternoon. *I never knew poetry could touch me so deeply*, she would say, her bronze skin warming him like a fever.

"Listen, Andrei." Dima ushered him into the office and offered a cigarette. "We need someone to run errands, and I thought of you. You'd pick up tickets, deliver ads, that sort of thing. It wouldn't pay much, maybe two hundred bucks, but you'd have the chance to move up in the company. Interested?"

"What about travel?" The salary was four times what he and Dima had earned at the research lab; Andrei felt the strain of ignoring this fact between them.

"For now, maybe some small discounts on tickets. But in time, if you become an agent, you could earn free trips." Andrei saw Dima take in his shaggy hair, his frayed jacket and jeans. "If you showed initiative. Ambition."

Andrei tried to picture himself in a suit and tie, planning a stranger's vacation on a computer. The image was ludicrous. "I'll think about it," he said, grinding his cigarette into a sleek black ashtray.

Dima looked through the glass wall and nodded. "You don't want to rush into anything." He stood up and extended his hand.

Andrei didn't mention his visit to the travel agency that night when Sveta came home late from work. Standing by the sink in her new blue suit and a pair of worn slippers, she ate the hot dogs and noodles he'd reheated for her. "I was thinking of inviting Melissa and Brad over for dinner," she said.

"You want to bring your Americans here?"

"Melissa wants us to cook a Russian meal for them."

"They've never had Russian food?"

"Don't you want to meet them?"

"Is there any reason I should?"

"What's that supposed to mean?" Sveta put her half-full plate into the refrigerator.

Andrei felt a rush of guilt, tinged with fear. He jumped up to embrace her. "It's the pleasure to meet you," he murmured into her ear in English. "My wife tells many incredible facts about you."

"Thank you," Sveta said primly. The *Santa Barbara* theme song was bleating in the other room. Her lips skimmed his neck, and she rose to leave.

The spring thaw arrived, bringing a week of heavy rain. Each morning Andrei rose with Sveta and prepared their tea while she bathed. When she was gone, he went back to bed and slept until lunchtime. Pavlova sat on the window ledge chasing raindrops down the glass with her paw.

On the morning the rain ended, Andrei left the apartment shortly after Sveta and took the train to the research lab.

"Our Andryusha has returned to the nest!" Lushin greeted him with a grin and a firm handshake, and they went to the cafeteria to smoke. "They finally paid us last week. Only a month's worth, though. They promised the rest soon, but I'll believe it when I see it."

"At least it's a start."

"You were right to leave. It's insanity."

"Do you think I could come back?"

"Come back?" Lushin laughed. "Why would you want to come back here? And don't tell me it's because you miss the work."

"If they're paying now . . ."

"If it's money you want, you should go into business like Dima."

"My wife is working for an American company."

Lushin nodded. "See? And does she like it?"

She's going to leave me, Andrei thought. "She likes it," he said.

"Well, there you are. Use her as your example, not an old granddad like me."

After he left the lab, Andrei walked to Novodevichy Cemetery and sought out graves: Chekhov, Gogol, Bulgakov. The air was damp and hazy; only a few foreign tourists wandered along the narrow stone paths, their heads buried in maps. Andrei was standing by Mayakovsky's grave, smoking, when a babushka groundskeeper walked up to him and leaned against her broom. She wore a faded dress bound by an olive-green sweater, and ragged gray sneakers.

"You know what he said." She angled the tip of her broom at the grave.

Andrei shook his head. "What?"

" 'Throw Pushkin, Tolstoy, and all the rest into the toilet.' Ha!" she snickered, displaying golden teeth.

Andrei exhaled a cloud of smoke.

"Nobody knows what to think of him now." Her face was smooth, almost untouched by wrinkles even when she squinted at Andrei. "But I guess *you* like him."

"You know what else he said?" Andrei dropped his cigarette into a puddle.

"Mm?" The woman's eyes were merry as she waited for the joke.

" 'She loves me? She loves me not? I wring my hands and scatter my fingers.' "

"Ha! I suppose his bones are rattling around in there by now. I suppose there's been time for that at least." She turned and walked away, her broom fussing at the path before her.

"You must be Andrei!" Brad Buckner's voice sent Pavlova slinking into the bedroom. He was a tall man with exquisite teeth and a firm handshake. "I've heard all about you!"

Melissa Phelps-Buckner slipped in behind him, carrying her

baby in a pouch like a mother kangaroo. "Hi, Andrei! I'm Melissa! And this is Brad! And this is Isabelle in here!"

"Yes, of course," Andrei said. "Please, to help . . ." He reached to assist Melissa with her coat, but it seemed inextricably bound with the baby and its carrying contraption.

"Oh, don't worry about that. Where's Sveta?"

"He is—" Andrei froze. "She is—" Melissa and Brad smiled at him expectantly. He rubbed his chin to indicate that he was thinking.

"Here I am!" Sveta said, emerging from the bedroom in the short red party dress she had sewn last summer. "Oi! It's Isabelle finally!" Andrei felt a surge of pride for his beautiful young wife. He longed for the night to be over, to slide the dress over her head. For months they had made love efficiently, like robots, but tonight he would make it last for hours.

The two women went into the bedroom to untangle Melissa from her baby. Andrei nodded at Brad to follow him into the sitting room, where the table was set for dinner. The room had doubled as Olga Vasilievna's bedroom when she was alive. Homemade bookshelves and cabinets filled with trinkets lined the walls; in a high corner, gold-inlaid icons glinted. "Please." Andrei pulled back the table and motioned for Brad to sit on the foldout couch.

"What a nice place! So cozy!" Brad displayed his beautiful teeth to Andrei as he leaned into the cushion. Andrei noted that Brad wore jeans and that his shirt was untucked. Sveta had bought Andrei a new tie for the occasion and made him wear his funeral clothes.

"May I offer you a glass of wine?" It was one of the sentences Andrei had memorized, and he was relieved to rid his tongue of it. He would mark the passage of the night by the number of sentences remaining in his head.

"What the hell! If you are, that is."

"Yes, of course." Andrei busied himself with the corkscrew.

"It's great to meet the man behind the woman." Brad laughed. "So to speak. Melissa's just thrilled with Sveta. She helps me out a lot, too. We think she's just great."

"Yes."

Brad accepted his glass and took a long drink. "I can't remember if Melissa told me what you do for a living, Andrei."

"A living?"

"You know, like, where do you work?"

"I work here. In the apartment." They nodded at each other for a long moment. "How do you . . . How do you like Moscow?"

"Oh, we think it's great." Brad shook his head. "I've been to Red Square, and it's stunning. Just stunning. So big, you know?"

Thankfully, Sveta appeared, carrying the baby in her arms, followed by Melissa. The baby was fat and pink, like any other baby. Andrei wondered when it would begin to look American.

"I love your place, you two!" Melissa said, beaming as she squeezed in beside Brad and nestled the baby into a padded plastic basket. Melissa's blue dress was drab and formless, and strands of wiry silver ran through her dull blond hair.

"It is small," Andrei ventured as he poured wine for the women. The apartment had never felt cramped before, even when Olga Vasilievna was alive, but now he felt as if the walls and ceiling were closing in on them.

"Small but cozy," Melissa said.

"A toast," Sveta said, raising her glass. "Andrei?"

"*Za udachnuyu rabotu,*" he said.

"I'll drink to that!" Brad said. "What's it mean?"

"To work," Sveta said.

"Oh, you just had to remind us!" said Melissa. "I propose a different toast: To friendship."

"To friendship!" Sveta cried. They all clinked glasses.

Andrei put down his glass. "Please, excuse me." He went into the kitchen and stared into the pot of borscht bubbling on the stove. That morning they had spent more than fifty dollars on food and wine. As they chopped and cooked, Andrei had become drunk on the abundance, the savory aromas, and Sveta's nervous excitement. Now he felt deflated and exhausted.

The dinner progressed from caviar and blini to soup, to roast veal and potatoes and greens. "This is wonderful! Best meal I've had since I got here!" Brad nudged his wife. The baby had dozed off in her basket. "Maybe Sveta could give you some Russian cooking lessons, Missy."

"Pretty soon Sveta won't have time for cooking lessons," Melissa said.

"Melissa has big plans for your wife, Andrei," Brad said.

"Oh?"

"I'd like to move her into personnel," Melissa said. "She has such wonderful people skills."

"What are they talking about?" Andrei asked Sveta in Russian.

"Melissa wants to train me for a new job," Sveta answered in English.

"What new job?" he asked. He felt ridiculous speaking English with his wife in public.

"Hiring employees," Sveta said. "It would be a wonderful opportunity for me."

"It would mean longer hours, but better pay," Melissa explained to Andrei.

"Maybe Andrei thinks Sveta works long enough hours already," Brad said. His lips were moist. Andrei had filled his glass many times, and each time, Brad had drunk the wine without waiting for a toast.

"The training would be in London," Sveta said as she bounced the baby on her hip. "Isn't that so, Melissa?"

"That's right. At international headquarters."

"London? For what time?" Andrei asked.

"Maybe a month," Melissa said.

"Why haven't you told me about this?" Andrei asked Sveta in Russian.

"It's not definite yet," she said, replying in Russian.

"You'd go to London without me for a month?" he murmured.

"If you worked for a travel agency, you could get a cheap ticket and visit me."

"I don't work for a travel agency."

"Oh, that's right. You're too busy writing poetry to work."

Melissa and Brad were staring at them. "I shouldn't have mentioned it," Melissa said.

"No, it's fine," Sveta said.

"Sveta's such a good cook," Brad said, "you can't blame Andrei for wanting to keep her to himself. Isn't that right, Andrei?"

"Yes," Andrei said. In his head, an image flashed: Olga Vasilievna's thick, chapped hand reaching to squeeze a loaf of bread on a store counter. He had never wanted his wife to be like her mother, but he didn't want an American wife, either. When they first met, he won over Sveta by playing his guitar. All he had ever wanted since then was to hold her admiration.

"So, Andrei," Melissa said. "Sveta tells me that you're a poet!"

Andrei stiffened. He had not memorized an appropriate response to such a statement. He looked at Sveta, but she was busy pouring more wine. "A little bit," he said.

"I'd like to hear some of it," Brad said, twirling his glass, the red wine glancing the rim. "You ever write in English?"

Andrei pushed back his chair. "One moment, please." In the dark bedroom, Pavlova's eyes shone metallic green from beneath the bed. Andrei returned to his seat with a dictionary and his notebook. Flipping past his doodles and sketches, he found a blank page and began to write.

"You know, you guys," Brad said, "ever since I came to Moscow, there have been these times when I look around me, and I think, holy shit! You know what I mean?"

Sveta smiled wanly.

"I mean, if my friends could see me now," Brad continued.

"I think tonight it's good they can't," Melissa said.

"Meaning what, exactly?" Brad said.

Andrei put down his pen and stood up, jostling the table. "This poem is to my wife," he said in English. He had Brad and Melissa's attention, but it was Sveta's he wanted. Finally she looked up, her eyes fearful.

He began to read:

> *"What filth, what filth, your people skills.*
> *My hands twist and my fingers crumble.*
> *O, Olga Vasilievna! Tonight*
> *she deny me*
> *three times."*

The room was as quiet as it had been before the guests arrived, as quiet as it was the morning Andrei found his mother-in-law dead on the very foldout couch where the Americans now sat looking from him to Sveta with wide eyes. Then the baby began to wail.

Andrei closed the notebook and sat down.

"I know just what you're talking about, buddy," Brad said, draining his glass.

Sveta scraped back her chair. "And now the dessert."

"It was very nice of you to share, Andrei." Melissa edged from behind the table and picked up her writhing baby. "Sveta, is there someplace I could feed Isabelle?"

"Please, the room where is our bed." She motioned toward

the hallway with the cake cutter. Her hand was trembling.

"Brad, I almost forget." Andrei brushed past Sveta to the cabinets. "The most important tradition of the Russian supper."

"I'll make the tea," Sveta said, then switched to Russian. "You sit down. You've done enough."

Ignoring her, Andrei revealed a bottle of vodka with a flourish.

"Now you're talking, Andrei!" Brad slapped his knee. "We're speaking the same language now!"

A scream sounded from the other room, high and raw. Another cry rose above it, then sunk into a growl as the first scream shook and climbed. Andrei, Sveta, and Brad stared at each other, frozen in wonder as the cries scraped against each other in jagged peaks. They moved down the dark hallway in a rush. One of the screams dropped, becoming a baby's wail. "Get it away!" Melissa cried, pushing past them, shielding the baby with her arms. Sveta and Brad followed her back into the sitting room. Andrei continued on.

Inside the bedroom, the cat's yowl rose and fell by octaves. The room was dim; Andrei switched on the overhead light and shut the door. Head lowered, ears pressed flat as arrows, Pavlova paced the far wall sideways. Fur stood in tufts on her humped back. When Andrei approached, the growl rose; she crouched and spit.

He sat down on the bed. Outside, he heard Melissa's muffled cries and Brad's droning voice. Pavlova slunk in narrow circles, her eyes fixed on Andrei. She fell silent; then she straightened. She approached Andrei and sat in front of him, tail swishing, eyes bright and eager. She was waiting for a piece of cheese, he realized.

Sveta came in and shut the door. Pavlova backed away and hissed, teeth bared. "What is wrong with you?" Sveta screamed at the cat. She turned to Andrei. "See what happens when you train a cat to do tricks?"

"What happened?" he asked.

"The cat attacked the baby." Sveta began riffling through papers on the desk. "Melissa was breast-feeding the baby, and the cat jumped up and bit the baby's foot."

"The cat was playing."

"Playing? It broke the skin—a terrible, deep bite. Melissa didn't even know we had a cat. It was dark, and she didn't know what it was; she was terrified. She screamed, and she said the cat just started leaping at them."

"The screaming must have scared the cat. She thought she was being attacked."

"They want to know if she's had shots. I told them we have a certificate."

"She was trying to defend herself," Andrei said. Pavlova had quieted again and was hiding behind the door of the wardrobe.

"Where's that damn certificate?"

"She hasn't had any shots."

"Here it is," she said, unfolding the tattered paper.

"That only says that some other cat's mother was a Persian."

"Well, they can't read it, can they?"

"Sveta." He tried to ease the certificate out of her hands, but Sveta jerked away, and it ripped.

"Look what you did!" she cried. "This is all your fault!"

"What are you talking about?"

"You trained our cat to be a monster!"

"Don't be ridiculous."

"You're glad she bit my friends' baby," Sveta said.

"Friends? They'll never be your friends."

Sveta stared at him, lips parted, eyes red and dark-rimmed. A sheen of sweat laced her skin. Andrei felt an empty desire, but he didn't want to touch her.

There was a knock on the door. Brad leaned into the room. "Hey, hi, you guys."

"Brad, I am so sorry." Sveta began to cry again.

"Hey, hey, don't worry, Sveta. It'll be all right. Listen, we're gonna go. We think we'd better take Isabelle to see a doctor. Just in case."

"I want to see Melissa," Sveta said, moving past Brad.

Brad shuffled into the room, unsteady on his feet. "Is your cat OK?"

"She is fine." Andrei motioned toward the closet door. "I will take her to the animal doctor tonight for the . . . examination. I will learn if she is healthy. And Sveta will say you the results."

"That's good of you." Brad held out his hand.

"It is . . ." Andrei measured his words carefully as they shook. "It is the very least I can do."

The emergency veterinary clinic was halfway across the city. It was late, and the train was almost empty. Every few stops, over the loudspeaker, a lilting voice asked respected passengers not to forget their belongings when exiting the train.

Pavlova had fallen into a deep sleep. Andrei kept his hand in the duffel bag beside him, encircling the cat's small body, a reassuring presence if she were to awaken and be frightened by the darkness and the noise.

OUR AMERICAN

The balcony was small, scarcely big enough for two stools, a stack of books, some empty flowerpots, and a broken washing machine the size of a television that Ilya and Sasha used as a table. It was a Monday afternoon in October, and they were eating blini, Ilya imitating his older brother, folding each pancake into quarters, swiping it in a bowl of cranberry preserves, and downing it in two bites. Ten stories below, boys played soccer in the long park that stretched out from the building. Treetops framed the soccer field on three sides; plumes of white smoke rose from the lumpy patchwork of orange and brown. The air was filled with the dark, bitter smell of burning leaves.

An hour before, a girl named Lena with long, honey-colored hair had shown up with groceries. Bustling and chattering, she fried the pancakes, served them to Sasha and Ilya, cleaned up after herself, and left. She was one of several girls, friends of Sasha's, who had been visiting the apartment in the month since Sasha returned from the army. Ilya didn't remember any of them from two years ago, but they remembered him, and they teased him about how much he had grown. "Pretty soon, Ilya," this one had said, "you're going to look just like Brad Pitt—only skinnier, and with glasses." Ilya was thirteen. Trying to imagine who he'd be when he stopped growing felt like trying to see the back of his head in a mirror.

Sasha wiped his mouth and let out a satisfied sigh. He was wearing his old blue jacket, jeans, and a pair of gray slippers that had belonged to their father. "That Lena, what a *baba*. She'll make a good wife."

"For you?" Ilya said.

"For you, maybe." Sasha smirked. "You heard her. She must like younger men."

Ilya tugged at a tuft of dead grass between two of the balcony's ceramic floor tiles, reaching to catch his glasses as they slid down his nose. Ever since Sasha appeared before Ilya and their mother on the train platform, tan and muscular, stubble dotting his gaunt face, his usual grin somehow lazier, more knowing, Ilya had felt shy of him.

Their father died of a stroke a few months before Sasha was drafted, and since then their mother had worked long hours at the bookstore. For two years there had been little for Ilya to do at home but anticipate his brother's return. When the second Chechen war started up midway through Sasha's service, Ilya began pasting newspaper articles and his brother's letters in a scrapbook. Neither the press nor Sasha told him much; the papers were full of vague reports about clean barracks and tightened borders, and his brother wrote only of the endless cold and damp. Ilya had been certain that when Sasha returned to Moscow, they would spend long hours drinking beer and talking about the war. He expected Sasha to curse Putin and his commanding officers and speak in grudging admiration of the rebels' fierce struggle for independence.

But instead of sharing his stories, or even looking for a job, Sasha spent his days dozing and reading the books their mother brought home: a biography of the American billionaire Bill Gates, and another by an American, Dale Carnegie, about making friends. Now he picked up the one on the top of the stack, a book about the power of positive thinking. Sasha burst out laughing as he read, finding the books funny in a way Ilya did not understand.

Their next-door neighbor Elmira Petrovna, an old Communist, came onto her balcony, which was separated from theirs by a low pipe railing and a sheet of tin. Letting her washbasin clang to the tile floor, she wrung out a piece of purple material from the top of the pile and stabbed it onto the line with clothespins. Ilya squinted at the fabric. He needed new glasses; it took him a moment to realize that the item on the clothesline was a brassiere. Much too small for Elmira Petrovna, he judged: the triangles of netting only slightly puckered, the straps slender as ribbons. Ilya could have hidden the whole thing in his fist. Sasha, Ilya noticed, had set the open book on his thigh and was also watching their neighbor.

"I've taken a boarder," the old woman announced without turning around. "An American girl."

"Elmira Petrovna!" Sasha said. "I thought you knew better than to mingle with foreigners—especially the kind that wear purple underwear."

"She's a good girl. She works on a collective farm."

Sasha grinned. "An American *kolkhoznitsa?*"

"She's a hard worker. Up every morning with the birds."

"Be careful, Elmira Petrovna," Sasha said. "Don't let her indoctrinate you into her capitalist ways."

"Hmph." The old woman retreated into her apartment, leaving a row of skimpy, brightly colored underclothes dripping onto her balcony. Sasha turned to his book again.

While Sasha was away in the army, Ilya had slept in his brother's bedroom and watched the dirty American movies that came on TV late at night. One was about a waitress who worked at a beach, delivering drinks to sunbathers. She wore a red bra like one on the clothesline and a long, flowered skirt with nothing beneath it. Right there on the beach, under a striped tent, the waitress had sex with two men at the same time.

"Have you seen her?" Sasha asked without looking up from his book. "The American?"

"No." Ilya hunched forward, letting his jacket cover the front of his pants.

"They say American girls are sluts." Sasha glanced at Ilya. "You know what that means, right?"

Ilya nodded.

Sasha smirked at his book. "Listen to this: 'If you say to yourself over and over, every day, *I want to be happy*, then you will soon find that you have more energy and ambition than you ever thought possible.'" He leaped to his feet. "I want to be happy!" he shouted. "C'mon, Ilya." Sasha pulled him up. "I want to be happy!" He nodded at Ilya, his brown eyes wide.

"I want to be happy," Ilya said quickly.

"No! Loud, like this: I want to be happy! I want to be happy!"

Drawing in his breath, Ilya shouted as loud as he could: "I want to be happy!"

"Me too!" a boy yelled from the soccer field.

Sasha and Ilya looked at each other and laughed.

"Boys! Do you want to be happy?" Sasha shouted.

"Yes!" Eight boys squinted up at the balcony.

"Here!" Sasha picked up the plate of leftover blini and tossed one of the pancakes into the air. The tan disk spiraled toward the boys. "Be happy!"

"Hey!" one of the kids yelled as the pancake landed on the dirt field.

"Eat! Eat!" Sasha threw more pancakes.

He passed the plate to Ilya, who flipped one into the sky. The boys staggered in circles, arms outstretched, whooping and yelling as the blini spun toward them.

"They're good!" one of them cried.

"Thank you, thank you!" the boys yelled.

"You're welcome!" Sasha shouted.

This was the Sasha Ilya remembered. One April Fool's Day, Sasha had rigged the showerhead so that it doused their father with a blast of icy water when he opened the bathroom door. While he stomped and spluttered and their mother chased him with a towel, Sasha and Ilya pranced around the kitchen, hooting with laughter.

"Bombs away!" Ilya shouted.

As quickly as the old Sasha had returned, he vanished again. The new Sasha put down the empty plate, slumped onto the stool, and closed his eyes. Within a minute he was softly snoring.

When Ilya got home from school the next day, Sasha was pacing in the driveway. Together they headed for the neighborhood market. Sasha had returned from the army knowing how to cook southern dishes with sharp flavors and funny names—*zharkop* and *chakhokbili*. Inside the cavernous market building, he stopped to inspect tomatoes being sold by two bearded men who spoke to each other in a foreign tongue. Ilya watched as his brother took a passport out of his back pocket and displayed the first page to the vendors. "Have you seen him?" he asked.

One of the men took the passport. " 'Goncharov, Nikolai Borisovich,' " he read. He looked at his companion. Ilya watched the three heads bent over the red booklet. Sasha's skin was lighter than the vendors', but they all had brown eyes and closely cropped dark brown hair. Sasha's stubble was filling out, becoming a sparser version of the men's neatly trimmed beards.

"Reminds me of Murat," one of the vendors said.

"What are you talking about?" said his friend. "Murat has big ears and blue eyes. This one has dark eyes, and his face is too long." He turned to Sasha. "Why do you think we would know him?"

"Never mind," Sasha said, reaching for the passport. One of the men offered to take down Sasha's phone number and ask around, but Sasha shook his head.

"Whose passport is it?" Ilya jogged to catch up as Sasha strode down the aisle.

"My friend Kolya's." He handed Ilya the passport. Kolya had a crew cut, thick eyebrows, and puffy, sullen lips. Born in 1980. City of residence, Omsk.

"He left it behind the night he disappeared," Sasha said. "I hid it."

"The government's talking about giving immunity to deserters," Ilya said, eager to show his brother all he'd learned. "But maybe he's a hostage. They're always looking to make trades. Sometimes they'll trade our guys for their guys, or for weapons. I even heard that—"

"How incredibly fucking interesting," Sasha said. He took back the passport and jammed it into his pocket.

Ilya fell back a step. How stupid, lecturing Sasha about the war.

"Come on." Sasha took Ilya's hand as if he were a little boy and pulled him forward.

When Sasha stopped to haggle for some chicken parts, Ilya found himself facing a cow's head that rested at the end of the long table. Maybe Sasha's laziness was just a ruse. Maybe he spent his days plotting to rescue his friend from captivity. Staring at the animal's dumb expression and pink ears, at the black crud stuck like tar to its nostrils, Ilya felt charged with expectation.

That evening, as they finished dinner on their balcony, the American girl burst onto Elmira Petrovna's, the suede hood of a forest-green *dublyonka* coat shrouding her face. She stood sniffling and blowing her nose. When Sasha coughed, she whirled around and lowered her hood. Her pink nose and cheeks emerged as if from a pool of water, the sun's last rays flaring in her dark curls. "Hi," she said, brushing dampness from her lashes. "I'm Amy."

As Sasha introduced himself and Ilya, she extended her hand over the railing, then withdrew it. "I forgot," she said. "Russian men don't shake hands with women, do they?" She had an accent, but made no mistakes.

"We don't?" Sasha raised his eyebrows.

"I could be wrong." She blew her nose. "It's just a stupid impression I formed at work."

"At the kolkhoz? You're picking up Russian customs from those hayseeds?"

Amy laughed. "That's not nice."

"You didn't learn Russian from them, that's for sure," Sasha said.

"My father's from St. Petersburg. Back in Ohio, it's our secret language."

"Was that why you were crying? Because you miss your parents?"

The wind picked up, and Amy held her hair back from her face. "I was crying because I don't have any friends here and I don't like my job. Plus, my driver just quit."

"Why didn't you say so?" Sasha said. "Ilya and I will be your friends. And I'll be your driver."

"I'd love it if you'd be my friends, but I need a driver who has his own car."

"Do I look like someone who doesn't own a car?"

She shook her head. "There I go, jumping to conclusions again."

"We've got one, don't we, Ilya?"

"Yeah," Ilya said. "But I don't have a license." They laughed. Ilya was glad Sasha mentioned the car. Their father bought the cream-colored Moskvich a year before his death, and during Sasha's absence Ilya had taken care of it—filling the oil, driving it around the building now and then. But the battery died in the summer, and someone had stuck nails into one of the tires. Ilya had asked his brother about getting it fixed, but Sasha hadn't shown any interest in the car until now.

Sasha stood up and slouched against the railing. Why shouldn't he be her driver?

The farm was an hour away, Amy protested, her hand on the door, and she was only going to be in Moscow until May. She couldn't pay much, either.

"I don't need much," Sasha said, "and we'll worry about May when we get there."

"I'm going to have to say no, OK?" Amy wasn't smiling anymore. She disappeared into the apartment, pulling the door closed behind her.

Sasha took out his rolling papers and tobacco. The sun was disappearing beneath the horizon of buildings, and Ilya tucked his hands under his thighs for warmth.

"She doesn't seem cheap, you know, like you hear people say," Sasha said, crouching forward as he shook a line of tobacco onto a square of paper. He rolled the paper into a tube and licked the edge closed.

Ilya thought Sasha had pushed Amy too hard, but what did he know about girls? Some of his friends bragged about fooling around, doing things to girls with their fingers and tongues in the woods behind school. Sasha was the only real man he knew.

"Why would an American girl live in a dump like this?" Sasha said. He lit the cigarette, one hand cupped around the trembling flame. He took a drag and passed the cigarette to Ilya.

Sasha had never asked his opinion about a girl before. Ilya sucked in an arrow of smoke and warmed his lungs, then shot it into the sky. "Maybe she wants to see what it's like," he said.

"Like an adventure, huh?" Sasha said, considering.

"Like going to the war," Ilya said, "except she can't, because she's a girl."

Sasha snorted. "Not to mention an American."

Ilya looked at his brother sidelong. "What about that passport? Are you going to give it to Kolya's family?"

"How would that help anyone?"

"I don't know." Maybe he could squeeze in one last question before Sasha changed the subject. "Do you think he's a deserter or a hostage?"

"What's the difference?" Sasha stared through the railing's bars. "He's screwed either way, unless he's dead."

Just one more. "Are you going to try to get him out?"

Sasha shook his head and laughed. "You really have no fucking idea, do you?" He got up and went inside, leaving Ilya alone with the cigarette, its smoke rising into the crisp air like a line drawn with chalk.

The following afternoon, the Moskvich was idling in the driveway, sparkling clean. "Jump in," Sasha said from behind the wheel.

"Where'd you get it fixed?" Ilya said after slamming the door.

"I found out where our American works," Sasha said. "We'll give her a ride home."

"But she said—"

"I'm not going to force her into the car. Anyway, she likes you, I can tell."

Ilya was glad to be useful, maybe for the first time since Sasha came home, and he felt relieved that his brother didn't seem annoyed with him anymore. He couldn't wait to see Amy. The night before, he'd thought about her as he fell asleep. He had a sense she would be good for him and Sasha, if they didn't mess things up—if they hadn't already.

The highway traffic was light, and Sasha drove fast, past open fields and birch groves—at first broken by rows of high-rise apartment buildings, then by dilapidated villages and new settlements of two-story brick houses. "No more cattle cars," Sasha said, staring straight ahead. This was their father's line, uttered proudly as they drove to the dacha during their final summer together as a family; the car had rescued them from the packed suburban trains. Ilya felt blindsided by happiness and longing, as if their father had swooped down into the driver's seat and vanished again.

At the turnoff for the collective farm, they bounced past fields overgrown with weeds as tall and thick as saplings. An old man leading a goat through the rusting gates pointed them toward the administration building at the end of a muddy road.

Amy looked up from her desk in the bright but sparsely furnished office and laughed. "Let me guess. You happened to be in the neighborhood?"

As they pulled onto the highway, Amy next to Sasha now, Sasha said, "I don't want a salary, as long as you buy the gas."

"What's the catch?" Amy said.

"If, by the end of the year, I've gotten you to work on time every day and haven't had any accidents, you have to buy Ilya a new pair of glasses."

Ilya tensed as if someone had trained a camera on him. Not wanting to burden their mother with the expense, he hadn't told anyone about needing new glasses. Sasha must have caught him squinting, maybe at Amy's underwear.

"Poor Ilya," Amy said, turning to frown at him. "You've got a deal." She shook Sasha's hand, then Ilya's. Ilya felt himself blush. Amy's hand was smooth and just about the same size as his own.

"There's the McDonald's," Amy said as they approached the city. "Elmira Petrovna likes it when I bring her home a cheeseburger." Sasha pulled off the road. Amy pointed him toward an arrow that guided them away from the parking lot. "Stop here," she said. They had come to a lighted menu board illustrated with photographs of sandwiches and drinks.

"What's this for?" Sasha said gruffly.

"Ilya and I will tell you what we want, then you tell the sign."

"A sign? I'm not talking to a sign," Sasha said.

"You're as stubborn as my father." Leaning over Sasha, Amy rolled down the window and braced her elbows on the door. Her hair pressed up against Sasha's scruffy beard, Amy shouted out their order. Then she directed Sasha to a window up ahead. He drove the car over the curb and swore under his breath. When he passed Amy's money to the cashier, one of the bills blew away. "Dammit," Sasha shouted.

Ilya dashed out of the car and chased after the bill. He knew about this restaurant from watching TV, but Sasha had been gone for two years. Amy wouldn't understand this. She would just think Sasha was being a jerk. He stepped on the bill.

The car was rolling forward. For a second Ilya thought Sasha was going to leave him in the parking lot, but the car stopped at the next window. Ilya jogged up to the first window and gave the bill to the cashier. Another car was creeping up behind him. He felt stupid, waiting on foot for his change.

"Fucking ridiculous," Sasha said when Ilya came back. A boy handed over the bags of food; the car instantly filled with the smell of fried potatoes. Ilya reached to take the bags from Sasha. Amy was staring out the windshield.

They had blown it. She would never like them now.

But at twilight three days later, Ilya looked up from a soccer game to see the Moskvich pulling into the yard, with Amy in the passenger seat. Upstairs, he found Amy, Sasha, and their mother, Alexandra, gathered in the kitchen. Sasha's bare arms and chest were covered with cuts and scratches, which Alexandra dabbed at with an antiseptic-soaked cloth.

"Your brother lost a fight with some thistles," Alexandra said to Ilya.

"He worked in the fields all day," Amy said.

"Just trying to help out," Sasha said. "Anyway, no point in driving back to Moscow."

"A city boy like you," Alexandra murmured. "You're a fish out of water on that farm."

"Where exactly do you think I've been for the past two years, Mama? Paris?"

"You'll have to get some decent gloves," she continued, "and wear an extra shirt and some long underwear."

"I'll make sure he does," Amy said. "The gloves, I mean."

"Let me get your sides," Alexandra said. Sasha raised his ropy arms, revealing two thatches of wiry hair. His ribs pulled away from his concave belly. "My God," their mother muttered. "Didn't they feed you anything in that war of theirs?"

"All the spuds we could dig. All the goat meat that bullets could buy." He winked at Amy. "Like eating at McDonald's every day."

Amy curled her lip at him. When had they made up? Ilya wondered. He and Sasha had sat shivering on the balcony most of the weekend, but Amy had never appeared.

Cutting a bandage into small pieces, Alexandra asked Amy if she had any brothers.

Amy shook her head. "Just an older sister."

"Your parents are lucky." Their mother's eyes filled. Her finger traced a thick purple scar that pushed against Sasha's back like a trapped worm. "Me, I'm twice cursed."

"They don't have a draft in America, Mama," Sasha said.

"Or a war," Amy said. "Not at the moment, anyway."

"Then *all* American parents are lucky," said Alexandra.

Ilya watched Amy's eyes dart over Sasha's body and settle on the scar. She returned Ilya's stare, her cheeks cherry red. Ilya felt off-balance, as if the building were swaying, as it sometimes did, in a strong wind.

A daily ritual began: Amy and Sasha sought out Ilya at the soccer field. Together they shopped for groceries, Sasha cooked, and they ate on the balcony. Sasha entertained them with imitations of the farmers at the kolkhoz, Amy, gasping with laughter, would order him to stop, insisting he was mean and cruel. Ilya loved how Amy laughed, soundless, shoulders shaking, tears streaming from her eyes. Once, when Sasha mimicked Amy trying to convince a drunken farmer to stop selling home-brewed vodka, she laughed so hard that milk came out of her nose. Sometimes, on the crowded balcony, Ilya's foot brushed against Amy's leg, by accident or on purpose. She seemed to like having him around—whether as a chaperone or as a second admirer, Ilya wasn't sure. As for Sasha's Russian girlfriends, they stopped coming by the apartment as mysteriously as Amy had reappeared.

Alexandra's store was undergoing a renovation, and she worked late taking inventory, often returning home after midnight. In the morning, Ilya would wake on the kitchen daybed to find his mother sitting across the table, already dressed for work, watching him in the grainy dawn light as she sipped her tea. They would exchange groggy smiles before his eyes fell shut again. An October frost finished off the last of the collective farm's weeds, and Sasha moved into the office, helping Amy with clerical tasks and learning to use the computer. "Building up my skills for a real job," he said, and Amy and Ilya nodded at his foresight, though none of them talked about what would happen when Amy's one-year posting ended in the spring. At night, eating side by side on the daybed, Amy would drape an arm over Sasha's shoulder, and when she did dishes at the sink, he sidled up and embraced her from behind. Ilya looked away, embarrassed by his own embarrassment but pleased by their growing affection. Sasha seemed more and more like his old self, fun-loving and eager, yet also more like a man who might someday speak with calm authority of his wartime adventures.

"A dangerous city, Moscow," Sasha would say when Amy headed for the door. "All the foreigners have bodyguards these days."

His insistence on walking her the two paces to Elmira Petrovna's apartment became their favorite running joke. "Check on us if I'm not back in five minutes," Sasha would say to Ilya, "and call the cops if we're not there."

"*Two* minutes, Ilya!" Amy cried, swatting Sasha's arm.

For a while, Sasha asked for ten minutes in the hallway. Then it was twenty. Ilya played along, tucking himself into bed, eyeing the alarm clock, marking the silent second they broke curfew, though he would never dare to seek them out. Elmira Petrovna didn't allow the boys in her apartment, so Ilya suspected Sasha made out with Amy in one of the elevators, leaving the door ajar to keep from being summoned to another floor. Maybe Sasha and Amy would get married. When Elmira Petrovna died, they could settle in the apartment next door, and Ilya could still have supper with them every night.

On Thanksgiving Day, the three of them sat down to eat a turkey so big it had barely fit in the oven; Amy had found it at a Swedish supermarket and seasoned it with spices her mother sent from America. Sasha opened the high window to cool the steamy kitchen. Ilya's nose untwined the dusky scents, pinning them down with the English words Amy had taught him: *nutmeg, sage, ginger*. As they passed bowls of mashed potatoes, bread stuffing, and carrot salad, Amy told Sasha and Ilya about the Pilgrims' feast.

"They wanted independence," Sasha said with his mouth full. "That's what they were fighting for, right?"

"Well, the fighting came later, but that's basically it." Amy paused with her fork in midair. "Kind of like your war, right?"

Ilya chewed quietly.

"When did they slaughter the aborigines," Sasha asked, "before the war or after it?"

"Native Americans. Hey, listen to me. The Chechens are fighting for freedom from Russia, and . . ."

"And if they keep it up, they'll be extinct, like your aborigines."

Amy frowned and pushed her plate away. "How come you never talk about it, Sasha?"

"What?"

"The war."

"Why should I?"

"It's not healthy to keep your feelings bottled up."

"You sound like one of those books Mama gave me."

"OK, so I'm American. I talk about feelings. So what?"

"Why would anyone want to listen to my stupid stories?" Sasha gazed from Amy to Ilya. His beard had caught a dribble of gravy. It had grown in thick and lush; the dark mustache drooped over his lip like moss. He looked even more like the men in the market, the rebels on TV. He could never get a real job with a beard like that, Ilya thought. It was just as well he worked at the farm.

"I'm sure you have fascinating stories to tell," Amy said.

Sasha made a face and bent over his plate again.

While Amy and Sasha cleared the dishes, Ilya took his war scrapbook out of the drawer of the daybed. Jittery, he opened it to the first page.

"What do you have there?" asked Amy, wiping the table. "

'Putin and Basayev: Showdown in Dagestan,' " she read, sitting down beside him.

"It's just a book I made."

"When did you do this?" Sasha said, looking down.

"While you were gone."

Amy read from a sheet of translucent paper lined with Sasha's small, neat handwriting: " 'Hello, dear Mama and Ilya. Greetings from the south. Can you read this? It's so dark I can't see these words.' " Amy looked up. "Do you remember writing this, Sasha?"

Sasha sat down on Ilya's other side and studied the letter. "I never wrote about what was really happening."

"I figured you didn't want Mama to worry," Ilya said.

Their eyes met. Why did Sasha look so young, despite his beard? It was his eyes, Ilya realized: Sasha looked frightened.

"Grozny," Ilya said, pointing at a picture of three blasted-out apartment blocks on a muddy street.

"I wasn't there," Sasha said. "We were in the villages, doing cleanup."

"Cleaning up what?" Amy said. She turned the page to some newspaper photos. In the first, two soldiers in camouflage slouched with their backs to the camera. Beyond their legs, bodies sprawled facedown, blending into mud. On the facing page, recruits were piled atop a personnel carrier, sitting on suitcases and canvas bags, some sneering at the camera, others grinning. Amy pointed at the television set on one of the soldier's laps and laughed.

"There's plenty of stuff to sell down there." Sasha's voice was low and soft. "Some of the things we sold weren't even things."

Ilya's heart thumped so hard he feared his shirt was moving. "What about your friend Kolya?" His voice came out cracked and high. "The one who disappeared?"

"You have a friend who disappeared down there?" Amy

said.

"He wasn't really my friend," Sasha said.

"What happened to him?"

"He was just a new kid." Sasha glanced at Ilya. "He didn't mean anything to me, but I didn't get involved. I wouldn't get messed up in something like that."

"Something like what?" Ilya said.

Sasha stared at him openmouthed.

"What are you talking about, Sasha?" Amy said. "Is he alive?"

"Maybe they traded him back." Sasha looked pleadingly at Ilya. "For one of their guys, like you were saying. It's not like they'd keep him forever."

Ilya nodded.

Amy rose from the table and turned on the tap. "It's really great, Ilya, that you wanted to learn about what Sasha was going through."

Sasha's head jerked toward her. "Yeah, it's really great, Ilya," he said, mimicking Amy's chipper voice, her schoolbook enunciation. "It's so downright American, making a cute little book to help us talk about our feelings." Shoving back the table, he pushed past Ilya, moved swiftly to his bedroom, and closed the door.

Amy turned from the sink with a quizzical look, as if someone had entered the room rather than left it. Without glancing at Ilya, she dried her hands on her long flowered dress and followed after Sasha.

That night Ilya dreamed he and his mother were refugees, running with strangers through a dark town from one abandoned house to another, twigs snapping underfoot. They huddled with some Chechens in a corner of a looted bedroom and covered themselves with blankets and discarded clothes. A soldier burst in, calling Ilya's name. Ilya opened his eyes. It wasn't a soldier looming above him, but one of the bandits, a dark gag binding his mouth. Ilya shouted, waking himself up enough to recognize Sasha, looking down at him, his beard only resembling a criminal's disguise.

"Shh," Sasha said. "Mama's sleeping."

Ilya sat up, drawing the blanket over his bare legs. His scrapbook thumped to the floor. "Where's Amy?" he whispered.

"At home in bed," Sasha said, reaching for the scrapbook. "Listen, you don't need to worry about it," he murmured, hefting the book in one hand like a rock. "You won't be going."

"Won't be going where?"

He put a finger to his lips. "To the army, stupid."

"Why not?"

"You'll go to America with Amy and me. When we get married."

"You're getting married?"

"Sure, why not?" The whites of Sasha's eyes shone like slivers whittled from the moon. "But don't say anything, for God's sake. Our American doesn't know yet. And stop talking about all that shit."

"But, Sasha—"

"Listen, don't worry. I like her, all right? She's a good girl." Frowning, he rubbed his beard. "The best I'll ever have, anyway, and I'll take care of her. But she can help us, too. Remember what Papa used to say?"

Ilya shook his head.

"Just as easy to fall in love . . ." Sasha raised his eyebrows.

"With a rich woman as a poor woman," Ilya finished. "Mama didn't like that one."

"That's because she was poor. Now listen," Sasha whispered. "It's the perfect plan. We won't let them get their hands on you." He unlatched one of the tall windows, letting in a wave of chill air. He peeled the first page out of the scrapbook as carefully as a strip of bark from a birch tree, and handed it to Ilya. "It's the best thing I could ever do for Mama."

"That's your letter."

"It's propaganda." Sasha flung the window open. "Put it where it belongs."

Ilya crawled to the end of the bed and held the sheet outside the window. It flapped, struggling like a bird, like his own heart thudding in his chest. He released the paper into the frigid night. It sliced the air, back and forth, then dove headlong, kamikaze-style, toward the trees.

Ilya had never feared for his own life before, but now that an invisible cocoon cushioned him from danger, his future in Russia seemed like a narrowly averted disaster. Alongside his brother's secret plan, Ilya's fantasy of Sasha and Amy moving in next door seemed hopelessly juvenile. Not only would Ilya stop asking Sasha about the war, he wouldn't even think about it.

Over supper, Sasha began to grill Amy about America. He wanted to know how much computer programmers earned in a month, whether it was true the best jobs were in California. One night, after twelve, Sasha and Amy put on their shoes and coats. Instead of bantering over the number of minutes Ilya should give them in the hallway, they left with nothing but hushed wishes for pleasant dreams. Ilya heard the elevator door slam shut, then the lurch and whir of the machinery, the chug of the cables. He arranged his pillow and blanket on the daybed, shed his jeans, and tucked himself in. Saturated with moonlight, the lace curtains etched milk-blue designs against the windowpanes. He imagined, down below, tendrils of frost evaporating into fog on the windows of the warming car. Ilya pulled back the curtain. Swirls of ice glazed the panes like waves on a stormy sea, obscuring the darkness beyond.

On a Monday morning in mid–December, Ilya and Amy hurried along the cobbled pedestrian mall, arms linked against the cold, passing caricature artists and souvenir salespeople stamping their feet for warmth. "Four more months of winter, right?" Amy said, her voice high and thin in the frigid air.

"Maybe five," Ilya said, pleased to find himself an authority on something, and to be walking arm in arm with Amy, even if there were few people to take notice of them on the Arbat today.

The optical store was warm and hushed, the walls lined with glasses and mirrors. The pretty young woman at the desk was expecting him; Amy had made an appointment, and Ilya was the only customer. She introduced him to another young woman, this one in a lab coat, who examined his eyes in a windowless room. Back in the display area, the first woman lightly touched his elbow, guiding him to the men's frames.

Ilya used to hate shopping for new glasses with his mother. They would traipse from one subway station to the next, seeking out the optical stands tucked by the stairs. Anyone rushing by could get a glimpse of Ilya trying on children's glasses until he found a pair that brought the world more or less into focus, always with chunky frames of mottled gray and brown. Now Ilya tried on one pair after another, basking in the female attention. He settled on a pair that Amy claimed made him look older. They weren't really frames at all, just a thin golden bridge and a pair of arms soldered to light plastic lenses. At the counter, Amy passed a credit card to the woman. The glasses, made especially for Ilya in Sweden, would be ready in two weeks.

Sasha had offered to pick up Ilya and Amy in the car, but they had finished early. They crossed the Arbat to Baskin Robbins and sat in the window eating ice cream.

"You look hot in those glasses, Ilya," Amy said. "The girls at school are going to be falling all over you."

"Nah." All the girls in his class cared about were American movie stars and bands like Ivanushki International. When they moved to America, he would find a girl like Amy—smart and cheerful and generous.

"You're going to be a real heartthrob in a year or two, I can tell. Just like your brother."

"The girl in the store was pretty," Ilya said to appease her.

She grabbed his hand. "I thought you liked her! And she thought you were cute, too. Did you notice how she kept brushing your arm?"

Amy's touch made him grow bold. "She's not as pretty as you."

"Aw," she said. They sat grinning awkwardly at each other, and then Amy's smile began to fade. She let go of his hand. "Ilya, there's something I want to talk to you about."

"What?" Maybe the compliment had been a mistake. Did she think he was in love with her?

"I haven't told Sasha this yet, but . . . I'm going to move soon."

"Into our place?"

"No. I mean, to another apartment in Moscow."

"What do you mean? Why?"

"It has to do with Sasha."

Ilya couldn't speak.

"The thing is . . . He has some pretty deep wounds, and"— she looked out the window—"and it's difficult enough for me, living here, without . . ." She turned to face Ilya. "Of course we'll still be friends. All of us."

"Are you still going to work together?"

She shook her head and picked up her ice-cream cup. "He'll have to find another job."

"Where?"

"God, Ilya, there are plenty of jobs in Moscow, and they all pay better than the farm!" Her pink plastic spoon fluttered through the air. "I mean, I'm sorry, but don't you think Sasha should contribute more to your family than just a pair of glasses once a year?"

Ilya fought back a surge of anger so strong it pushed tears to his eyes. "You paid for the glasses, not Sasha."

"It's his salary, Ilya. Remember?"

Ilya looked out the window. He'd been pretending that today was a gift from a friend, a member of the family, even. Already he had begun to view Amy as someone from whom kind gestures, even extravagant ones, could be accepted casually, without thought of payment due or favors traded.

There was Sasha, striding toward them.

"It's not like we've been together all that long, Ilya." Amy got up and wound her scarf around her neck. "You'll understand better when you're older."

When they were outside, Sasha bent to kiss Amy on the cheek. They headed down the nearly deserted mall, falling into the same stride, three plumes of breath preceding them. Amy gushed insincerely—Ilya saw this, now—about how handsome he looked in his new glasses. The laughter Sasha returned was phony, too, as if he had learned the ideal tone and duration from his book about making friends. Had this falseness been between them all along?

A young policeman in a gray coat and hat stood at the end of the sidewalk, across from the McDonald's. He was staring straight at them, and when they approached, he tapped Sasha's arm with his billy club. "Papers," he said. "You too," he said to Amy. He ignored Ilya.

"Is there a problem?" Amy asked as she dug through her purse.

The officer didn't say anything. Sasha reached into his back pocket and handed over a passport. What if Sasha had given Kolya's passport by mistake? Ilya wondered. He had seen two red passports on Sasha's dresser, placed side by side, their covers indistinguishable. Then Ilya had a strange thought: What if Sasha handed over Kolya's passport on purpose?

The officer studied the passport for a long time, leafing through it page by page. While Sasha was away, Ilya often saw the police stop dark-haired, dark-skinned men from the south. He felt a thrill when he passed one of these scenes, wondering if the detained man was a terrorist, certain his brother was working to make the streets of Moscow safe. Ilya studied Sasha. His knit cap was pulled down to his eyebrows, his beard thick and wiry. He looked at the ground as if hiding guilt. Ilya saw what an idiot he was to have believed Sasha's plan. He wouldn't marry Amy; they wouldn't go to America. The only thing Sasha was right about was the war. It would start up again, and Ilya would put in his time and come back as screwed-up as his brother was, or he'd end up like Kolya, and never come back at all.

The policeman handed back Sasha's passport, then glanced at Amy's blue passport and visa. "Thanks," he said, retreating a step.

"I should get one of those," Sasha said, nodding at Amy's passport. They veered onto a side street canopied with snow-laden trees. "I've never heard a cop thank anyone."

"What was that about?" Amy asked.

"It's because of Sasha," Ilya said.

"What?" Amy said.

"He looks like a terrorist."

"A terrorist?" Amy frowned.

Sasha stopped in front of the car. "Like a Chechen, you mean?"

"Yeah," Ilya said. He was surprised to find himself short of breath, puffed up with indignation. "You even dress like them."

Sasha turned to Amy. "Do you think I look like a Chechen?"

"How should I know? I've never even seen a Chechen," she said. "Look, it's freezing. Can we go home?"

"Wait a minute." Sasha faced Ilya, arms crossed, feet apart in the snow. "Why would I want to look like a terrorist?"

"I don't know. Maybe you're ashamed."

"Ashamed of what?"

"Of what you did down there. That's why you don't want me to be a soldier, right?" Sasha shook his head almost imperceptibly, and Ilya understood what he had said, and what his brother feared he'd say next. Once he knew, he couldn't stop himself: "That's why you want to marry Amy."

Amy and Sasha froze, staring at Ilya. For the first time, he felt the full, dizzying force of their mutual attention.

"What was that, Ilya?" Amy asked in a small voice.

Sasha clutched Ilya's jacket and pulled him forward. "Shut up," he said, lips parting in a snarl. His breath smelled like mustard.

"Sasha, let go of him," Amy said. "What did you say, Ilya?"

"Sasha wants us to move to America with you."

"Very funny, Ilya," said Sasha.

"What are you talking about, Ilya?" Panic rose in Amy's voice. She was backing away. "Tell me, Ilya. Tell me now!"

"He wants to marry you so we can leave, so I won't have to join the army."

"Liar!" Sasha pushed him, and Ilya reeled backward, slamming against the car.

"Leave him alone!" Amy grabbed Sasha's sleeve, but he shrugged her away.

"It's not true!" Sasha shouted at her.

Catching his breath, Ilya rose to his feet. He didn't need Amy to defend him. Whether she knew it or not, she had led them on, made them dream of a life free from worry and loss.

And Sasha, stupid Sasha, still believed in that dream.

"He thinks you're a slut!" Ilya shouted. He buried his head in his arms and held his breath.

Sasha kicked Ilya in the thigh, hard, then in the gut. Ilya fell to the snow and rolled onto his side. "It's not true!" Sasha yelled. "I never said that, Amy! He's fucking lying!"

"You asshole!" Amy screamed. From the ground, Ilya watched Amy tug at Sasha's arm. He pushed her away, and she stumbled backward. "I knew you were fucked up!"

"It's a lie!" Sasha shouted. "I swear!"

Ilya looked up. Sasha was panting hard. "Ilya, tell her." He punched Ilya's arm. "You know it's a fucking lie."

Maybe it was a lie, but it would protect Sasha from the benevolent pity Amy had bestowed upon Ilya with his ice cream.

"Tell her," Sasha hissed. "Tell her it's a lie."

"Are you OK, Ilya?" Amy's voice was growing faint.

"Amy, come on," Sasha yelled, laughter in his voice.

"Fuck you," she screamed in English. Ilya could see her backing away, pointing at Sasha. "I hate you!"

"Amy, I swear! He made it up!"

"Stay away from me!" She turned and began to run.

"Get in the car," Sasha growled at Ilya, yanking him to his feet.

Ilya broke loose and dodged his brother. He staggered in the direction Amy had headed, but the street was empty. Sasha wasn't following him. Ilya cut over to the Arbat and leaned against a building. Wheezing, he cradled his knee and tried to catch his breath. In the middle of the snowy mall, a small woman with white-blond hair sat in a director's chair, her fur coat and sweater pushed down to bare her narrow shoulders. She was posing for an artist who was bundled in a parka, his gloved hand traveling swiftly over the sketch pad. From this distance the page was only a blur of gray to Ilya. Swallowing back a sob, he turned and began to limp down the silent street.

Someone was banging on a neighbor's door. Silence; then a key turned. Ilya sat up and reached for his glasses. Seeing his brother's shadowy figure stumbling into the dark apartment, Ilya made his way to the hallway on sore legs.

"Whaddya want?" Sasha lurched into the living room. Ilya followed him.

"Sasha?" their mother said sleepily from the foldout couch.

"Go back to sleep, Mama," Sasha said. He crossed the room and fumbled with the latch on the balcony door.

Ilya grabbed his brother's arm. Sasha pushed him back and threw open the door. A gust of frigid wind blew in; a high wedge of snow crumbled onto the parquet floor. Sasha stepped onto the balcony. Ilya grabbed his arm.

"Lemme go," Sasha said, and flung him against the door-jamb. As Ilya struggled for balance, Sasha climbed over the divider and fell onto Elmira Petrovna's balcony.

"Sasha, what are you doing?" their mother called from inside.

Sasha rose to his feet and began to pound on Elmira Petrovna's window with his fists. "Amy!" he yelled, his voice filling the night. "Amy, come here!"

Ilya eased himself over the railing and grabbed his brother from behind. Sasha's body was like a tree trunk, his arms flailing against the window like branches in a blizzard.

"Amy!" he cried. "Amy, I'm sorry!"

"Sasha!" Their mother shouted from the doorway in her bathrobe. "Get back here!"

A light came on. Elmira Petrovna stood at the far end of the narrow room in a white nightgown, brandishing a long knife. "Go away!" she screamed, her voice muffled through the window. "I'm calling the police!"

Sasha stopped pounding. "I just want to talk to Amy!" he shouted. "Tell her to come here!"

"The American's not here, I tell you! She went to a hotel! Go away! Go away!"

"I need to talk to Amy!" Sasha shouted. "I have something to tell her!"

"She's not there," Ilya said, his arms wrapped tight around his brother's chest.

Sasha went limp. Ilya fell back against the divider, and Sasha fell on top of him, pressing him into the snow. Ilya wriggled until he could breathe freely. As his brother's body warmed him, Ilya stared up at the dark blue sky, the edges tinged with light like cracks in a tent.

"I wanted to tell her something," Sasha said, huffing.

"What?"

"Just something."

Their mother was shouting at them to get up.

"Is it about your friend? Is it about Kolya?"

Sasha made a choking noise.

Ilya pressed his cheek against Sasha's damp neck. He had waited all this time for them to be close, and he was ready. Amy had brought them together, but they did not need her anymore. "Tell me."

Sasha's head slumped against Ilya's shoulder. "Nothing," he said.

Ilya was skating on the iced-over soccer field when he heard a girl calling his name. She stood at the edge of the low corrugated wall in her *dublyonka* coat, cheeks flushed, hair pulled back. She looked Russian, but when he skated over, he saw that she was smiling, and she became American again.

"You're pretty good," Amy said. "I tried skating last week, and it was a disaster. It's those Russian skates—no ankle support."

He looked down at his skates, feeling bad that he had not missed her.

She asked about Sasha, and Ilya told her that he was working the night shift at a printing company. "I don't see him that much," he said.

"I'm glad he found another job." Amy reached into her pocket and handed him a small rectangular case made of black leather. "Happy New Year."

He shook his head.

"Ilya, come on. They were made for you."

The case was hinged like a box. Inside, the glasses were almost invisible against the black velvet. Ilya handed her his old glasses. The new ones were light; the arms snapped open with a precise click. He put them on and looked at Amy. She looked the same.

"What do you see?" Amy said.

Ilya turned. The rungs on the ladder of the children's slide were corroded with orange rust. A nearby streetlight was decorated for the new year with garlands of silver tinsel, and the individual strands looked as sharp as wire. The ice behind him was rutted and coarse. Boys raced by, slashing strokes of white.

Ilya peered up at the building through the delicate tangle of tree limbs. He thought he found their balcony, then realized he was looking at the one below theirs. He tilted his head back and stared at the slender black branches that crisscrossed the building like a net frozen in the sky.

THE YOUNG PEOPLE
OF MOSCOW

Flurries of cottony fluff swirl through the air, spinning into tornadoes, buffeted by traffic on the jammed boulevard. Young Muscovites in business suits, their eyes shielded by sunglasses, brush by Nina and Vassily as if the two of them are statues. Freshly hatched from their building's dark vestibule, heads tilted skyward despite their heavy loads, she and her husband probably do resemble an old-time monument, Nina thinks: a stone tribute to Soviet pensioners, dumbstruck by the glorious future that awaits even them. *Ever forward!*

"A blizzard," Nina says, glancing at her husband.

"A blizzard in June!" Vassily crows. He is an elfin man, short and sturdy, with red-white hair that sprouts in tufts. "Ninochka, darling . . ." His voice turns gentle as he smiles at his wife. "It's simply *pukh* from the poplars." Shifting his rucksack of books to both shoulders, he pivots, launching their journey.

"Of course." Nina hurries after him, the fold-up table braced under her arm. "How silly of me." She's relieved that he passed her little test, but she feels guilty, too. Lately, one or two mornings a month, Vassily keeps his distance and calls her *Tiotya*—Auntie—perhaps thinking himself a bachelor once again, who has come upon a lunatic old woman puttering in his apartment. Sometimes Nina suspects it is the absence of rhyming that has dulled his mind. Five years ago Vassily quit writing poetry, as if retiring from an ordinary job—welder or mail carrier.

"Interesting, those poplars," he says. "We used to have greening campaigns in Moscow, coinciding with the great building projects. I myself transported seedlings from Peredelkino to the capital, holding them in a pot on my lap on the train." He's been repeating this story ever since the first puff drifted through the open window two days before. "Perhaps I myself am to blame, in my small way, for the excess of female poplars in Moscow."

The boulevard groans with traffic—Ladas and Zhigulis shadowed by Range Rovers and Mercedeses. Across the street, Children's Goods sports a new glass-encased staircase and a brightly colored sign. Nina allows her thoughts to lift, electric as the downy seeds. Why shouldn't she daydream, too? Squinting, she imagines it is late December: strands of lights linking streetlamps, white and silver Yule trees behind fogged plate glass, snow. One New Year's Eve when their marriage was young, they came home from the Writers' Union party tipsy from champagne and rich hors d'oeuvres. Vassily undressed her by the window—why they were in the kitchen, Nina can no longer recall. She faced the darkened windows of the children's store, naked.

She thinks of the American couple she saw clutching each other on television the night before. When the news program came on, Nina had been sweeping fluff onto the balcony; Vassily was visiting his friend Ivan upstairs. Hearing the American woman explain through a translator that she and her husband had adopted a baby from an orphanage in Moscow, Nina set aside her broom and sank into the armchair. Soon after they took their new daughter home to New York, Mrs. Wolters told the Russian reporter, they realized she had severe brain damage. She screamed incessantly; she would never speak or

walk. They decided they could not raise her, nor could they afford to place her in a facility in New York, Mr. Wolters
claimed, so they returned the baby to the Moscow orphanage.
At the end of the interview, Mr. Wolters stooped over his wife
as she hid her face in her hands and cried.

That night, while Vassily whistled beside her in his sleep,
Nina cried, too. Inside her head, she began to compose a letter.

Dear Mrs. Wolters,

Last night I saw you on a television program in
Moscow, talking about your baby. I am writing to you
because many years ago I was in a similar situation. In
June of 1967, I gave birth to a baby girl. The doctor
knew immediately that our daughter was not normal.
Some of her features were unusual, her nose and her
forehead, though she had soft red hair like my husband.

The doctor urged us to put Dasha in a children's
home, as is the custom here. My husband agreed, but I
resisted. I could guess how our daughter would be
treated in such a place, and there was no chance she
would be adopted. But after several days I relented. I
hoped for another child to erase my memory of Dasha.
Six months after her birth, we received a letter from the
orphanage telling us that she had died of pneumonia.
We never had another child.

On this bright morning, Nina's desire to reach out to the
American woman strikes her not only as impractical—how
could she ever learn her address?—but sentimental, foolish.
Mrs. Wolters had conned Nina with her tears. She had taken
another woman's child abroad, then returned her like flawed
merchandise. For Nina there was no choice. She reconciled
herself to this fact long ago.

"And so, each year," Vassily is saying, "Moscow is assaulted by *pukh* from the female poplars, and my allergies . . ." He grimaces, as if his forgetfulness carries a sour taste. "But I don't get allergies like I used to, do I?"

"The medicine, Vasya?" Just ten minutes ago Nina set one half of an imported pink pill on his quivering tongue. She wards off his red eyes and his sneezes with just half the recommended dosage, stretching one box of the expensive medicine through the whole season. Spurred by this triumph, she hunted for an American remedy for memory lapses, but if such pills exist, they have not yet landed in the pharmaceutical kiosks of northeast Moscow.

"More like confetti, really, than snow," Vassily mutters, hands shading his eyes. He must be remembering the old-time parades: tanks creaking down streets lined with flag-waving Young Pioneers. On these holidays, a chauffeured Volga would drive them to programs at Palaces of Culture throughout the city.

Now they reach the cement square in front of the pillared metro station, an open-air bazaar of striped and polka-dotted tents. Flimsy tables bow beneath the weight of imported toothpaste and laundry detergent, loaves of bread, bouquets flown in from Holland. Newspapers scream of theft and mayhem. There are high stacks of books, too; on the covers, buxom women embrace men whose shirts billow open like curtains.

Vassily halts, nose in the air. Nina knows he would prefer to spend the day above ground, amid the cellophane-wrapped roses and the steam of plump sausages wafting from the German food trailer. But down below, the foot traffic is better, and they will be sheltered from the toylike police car that barrels through the square, scattering merchants like chickens. When Nina jerks her head toward the steps of the pedestrian underpass, Vassily follows without protest.

The light slips away as they descend; Nina fits the soles of her tennis shoes against the metal rods where the concrete has worn away. She hears the women before she sees them. Their voices bloom gradually, as if from her own television set, warming up:

"Real American sneakers . . ."

"Parisian stockings . . ."

"Toy trucks from Finland . . ."

The women flank both walls of the tiled tunnel, holding up toys and clothes: dumb-faced stuffed animals, synthetic blouses, stiff taffeta dresses for little girls. The plush and plastic absorb the tunnel's meager light, leaving the women's eyes rimmed with purple shadows. They are middle-aged, with matted hair-dos, and mouths that twist and grimace. To Nina the women look demented: hags clutching children's things, calling each other to play.

The one with the pockmarked skin is rooted in Nina and Vassily's spot again, brandishing a leopard-print sweater snarled with golden thread. Shuffling into position, Nina nudges the woman to the left. Vassily drops the bag of books to the ground and freezes beside her.

Nina snaps down the table legs and begins to arrange the books in a configuration she has designed to attract customers. The red-covered book of nature poems goes in the center, the piles of blue books on either side; red and blue are the colors of both the American and the new Russian flags, and thus suggest modernity. The remaining three stacks—books bound in still pungent leather, brown and forest green, branded with Vassily's name in a cursive typeface one never sees anymore—hide in the back row. She straightens the price tags and props up her hand-lettered sign.

GREAT RUSSIAN POETRY
REASONABLY PRICED!
PERSONALIZED INSCRIPTIONS BY THE POET
FREE OF CHARGE!

A WONDERFUL GIFT FOR A SCHOLAR
OR FOR ANYONE YOUNG AT HEART!

Nina laces her fingers and composes her face into the humble, kindly expression she hopes will remind passersby—young people rushing to work, mothers leading their children from the metro station to Children's Goods across the street—of their aging mothers. In fact, several women have bought a copy of Vassily's nature poems for an elderly parent. Most, however, quicken their pace after glancing at the old-timers standing silent, stubborn guard over the rubble of molding books, or fail to notice them at all.

The books had crowded their wardrobe for years. Each time a new one was released, Vassily received a few boxes and doled out copies to his friends. A month ago, unable to cram their winter coats back into the wardrobe, Nina lifted a box of leftover books and ordered Vassily to get the door.

"Throw them out?" Vassily cried. "Are you mad, woman? These are perfectly good books! We should be selling them!"

Nina seized on the idea. The regime Vassily served loyally throughout his career had also recently retired. Nina's and Vassily's pensions had diminished, and without his writing to tend to, the days proved difficult to fill. A project might stave off his decline. So Nina made her sign and let Vassily bluster about, knocking on the doors of his few living friends, phoning the Writers' Union, *Pravda*, and even the television stations to request press coverage. But when Nina led him to the underpass and he saw what selling his poetry on the open market required, Vassily's eyes dulled. He rarely speaks when they are in the tunnel, although when someone buys a book, he cheerfully asks for a name and writes an effusive inscription. His wild script always surprises Nina, his former typist, like an old familiar voice on the telephone.

Nina tries not to begrudge the other saleswomen their

smug stares. Though a full generation behind her and Vassily, they are not young enough to know how to succeed in this new world. Nina hears the gossip—the women's whispers echo through the tunnel as distinctly as their cries. The one across the way, for instance, with the plum-tinted hair and thin lips. One day in April her husband leaped from the balcony of their tenth-floor apartment building. She has two boys at home.

Perhaps Nina was too harsh in her judgment of the American couple the night before. She picks up the imaginary letter to Mrs. Wolters where she left off.

> Certain Russian doctors and politicians insulted you on television, Mrs. Wolters, saying that you are the reason foreigners should not be allowed to adopt our babies. In truth, very few Russian families would try to raise such a child. Nor would we speak on television of the children we have given away.

Across the tunnel, a man in a brown leather jacket is haggling with a woman for a toy car. After handing over some money, the man balances his briefcase on his knee, tucks the hot-pink convertible next to a liquor bottle, and hurries off.

Nina remembers an item she saw in the newspaper a week ago. An artist baked a life-size sponge cake of Lenin lying in state, and a gallery in central Moscow held a party and served the cake to journalists and guests. Nina imagines a crowd of young people stuffing cake in their mouths, snapping photographs, roaring with laughter. Though she was never passionately devoted to any leader, the irreverence unsettles Nina. If given the chance, the young people of Moscow would consume not only Vladimir Ilyich but her and Vassily as well. More than the lack of rhyming, she decides, this loss of respect explains Vassily's reluctance to inhabit the present.

My husband, Vassily, was never a famous writer, Mrs. Wolters, but his career gave us small opportunities—a summer home at Peredelkino, privileges at the Beriozhka store. We were married many years before I finally became pregnant. Vassily was so excited, he wrote a book of children's verse.

Do you suppose it would have been published if we kept Dasha? We were almost middle-aged by then. Vassily had no other trade, and I could only type. We had to protect our future.

The children's book was his biggest success. Some of the poems were reprinted in schoolbooks, and one was even made into a cartoon. Our copies are all gone, but the others we sell, several each week, enough for a decent cut of meat. When I slip a few bills into Vasya's wallet, he surprises me with bouquets of wildflowers.

Nina looks up at the ceiling, where water stains bloom in patterns already familiar to her.

I can't help but wonder, Mrs. Wolters, what would have become of us if Vasya had been a great poet—the type of poet who would not have been published here. Perhaps we too would be living comfortably in New York City. Perhaps we would celebrate Dasha's thirtieth birthday this year.

"Welcome!" Vassily shouts. He rushes from behind the table, arms flailing, toward two young men striding through the tunnel.

"Vasya," Nina calls, panicked. She had expected his madness to creep up on them slowly, like vines. But in this instant she reconciles herself to outbursts, handcuffs, a hospital for the insane.

Not daring to leave the books unattended, she watches Vassily grab one of the men by the arm as if he is an old friend. Tall, with dark, rippled hair, dressed in a checked suit, the young man looks like no one they could know. His companion, unshaven and rumpled, balances a bulky video camera on his shoulder.

"What do you want, Uncle?" The tall man pauses in front of the table. He is holding a microphone: a reporter, though he can't be more than twenty-five. Nina understands and almost laughs. With a last glance at the books—does she expect they'll fly away?—she joins her husband's side.

"We've been waiting for you!" Vassily cries, shaking the reporter's arm with vigor.

"What's the fuss?" the man says, frowning.

"Allow me to introduce my husband," Nina says, "the respected poet, Vassily Petrovich Musakov."

"My pleasure." The reporter raises his eyebrows at the cameraman. "We've got an appointment, but—what exactly are you doing down here, anyway?"

"My husband is selling his poetry." Nina fans her hand over the table. She imagines the Wolters watching her smooth gesture on television while an actress recites her words in English. "These are his books. You understand, these are difficult times."

"I take it your husband made a good living in the past?" the reporter asks.

"Oh, yes. We had no complaints."

The reporter thumbs through the book of nature poems, reading titles out loud: " 'The Ever-Flowing River.' 'To D. I. Mendeleev.' " He looks at Vassily. "You wrote these?"

"Yes, indeed," Vassily says. "Most of them before you were even born, I imagine!"

"All right, then," the reporter says, clapping Vassily on the shoulder. "Someday we'll have a nice long chat about your fascinating life."

Vassily grips the man's shoulder. "You're not leaving before the recitation, are you?"

"The recitation?"

"My husband would be honored to read some of his verse for you," Nina says. How Vassily used to love an audience! With his booming bass and fiery presence—his red hair dancing like a flame—he could hold an entire auditorium spellbound. Who knows what might happen if he could feel such power again?

The reporter looks at his partner, who shrugs. "You'll have to be quick, Uncle. No epics today, understand?"

Vassily scans the red book's index. " 'The Ever-Flowing River'—you say that's your favorite?" he asks, flipping through the pages.

"Sure, Uncle. Sure it is. Ready now?"

Without warning, a white light blinds Nina. She backs away and watches as Vassily slides a comb through his hair. The women's cries have subsided; only coughs and whispers echo through the tunnel. They never would have guessed the old man with the ancient books was important enough for television.

"This is Simeon Shustov, reporting from a pedestrian underpass in northeast Moscow," the reporter says into his microphone. "I have here Vassily Petrovich Musakov, once a highly privileged national poet, now a destitute pensioner selling his books in the belly of the capital. Vassily Petrovich, please tell our television viewers how you arrived at such dire circumstances."

"Well, you see," Vassily says, leaning into the mike, "it is important for a poet to be a man of the people. If he loses touch with the proletariat, his verse will ring false. He must constantly strive for authenticity, for simplicity, and, above all, for community."

"I see. And let's ask your wife . . ."

Nina edges into the light and introduces herself.

"Nina Mikhailovna, what do you make of your situation?"

"Vassily Petrovich and I never expected to find ourselves selling his books on the street. We try to be optimistic, but it's difficult."

"Tell me, how many books do you sell each day?"

"Quite a few, because you see, while the state has forgotten Vassily Petrovich, the people have not."

"And now," Shustov says, "Vassily Petrovich Musakov will share some of his verse with our television audience."

Vassily closes his eyes, composing himself. The strong light bleaches his skin, and Nina thinks, This is what he will look like in his coffin.

" 'The Ever-Flowing River,' " he bellows into the microphone, and begins:

> *"From the bulwark of the majestic steamer*
> *A sleepless sailor ponders the mighty Dnieper . . ."*

Vassily's sweeping hand gestures and sonorous voice, speckled with trills, are just as hearty now as they were decades ago. But imprinted upon an old man with quivering jowls, the youthful affectations are unseemly. The poem, meanwhile, has declined at the same pace as its author. The women's mocking whispers simmer beneath his words like the hisses and snags of an old phonograph record. Vassily himself sounds like the actors on the albums he used to bring home from union meetings, overwrought orations of Lenin or Brezhnev he'd play once, out of respect, before shelving for eternity. His eyes dart suspiciously, detecting the unrest. How ridiculous of Nina to expect a triumph that would shake Vassily out of his fog. This embarrassing spectacle won't be shown in New York or even on the evening news—unless to amuse the young.

When a high laugh rips through the third stanza, Vassily's voice sputters to a halt. He shields his eyes with his hand, surveying his audience.

"Is that all, Uncle?" Shustov calls out.

"No . . . not all." Vassily's gaze flutters across the tunnel and settles on Nina, beseeching.

Was he under the impression he was back in Sokolniki Park, encircled by a carefree holiday crowd? Has he truly not noticed, all these years, what has become of them? Nina closes her eyes, shutting him out. She sees little girls in sailor dresses, fidgeting cross-legged on a grassy field. Little girls who for decades have been women.

Shustov is clearing his throat, but Nina beats him to the first word. "Perhaps the audience would prefer one of your children's poems, Vassily Petrovich," she says. " 'Gathering Berries with Nastya,' maybe?"

"Ah . . ." Vassily squints. "Yes, perhaps . . ."

"This poem was quite popular in the sixties," Nina tells Shustov.

"Is that so?"

"Oh, yes. We don't even have any copies of the book left, but Vassily Petrovich has it memorized, don't you, Vassily?" His head bobs uncertainly. "Nothing is nicer . . ." she prompts.

"Nothing is nicer," he echoes.

"When we're at the dacha," she continues.

"When we're at the dacha," he agrees, and then his face turns to granite.

"You remember the next lines, don't you, Vassily Petrovich?"

He shakes his head, eyes pleading. But when she continues, he joins in:

"Than gathering berries
With big sister Nastya."

Nina's voice fades away. Vassily carries on alone, his voice hoarse and pinched.

> *"I follow behind,*
> *Swinging my pail*
> *While Nastya seeks out*
> *The well-worn trail."*

The whispering starts up again, higher and steadier, as if the women hide cicadas within their palms, but Vassily never lifts his wide, haunted eyes from Nina. She forbids herself to blink. In thirty-nine years this is her first true betrayal, and she savors it on her tongue like a dab of red caviar, letting the salty bubbles pop and melt one by one.

The spring she was pregnant, they took morning walks in the Peredelkino woods, the sound of clacking typewriters carrying them from one cottage to the next. In the afternoons Nina took dictation, resting her forearms on her firm, round belly as she typed. It was the baby that inspired him to switch to children's verse, Vassily told her, stooping to enfold her in his arms.

> *"Here the bushes are thick*
> *And the berries so rare*
> *That I start to worry*
> *We'll meet up with a bear."*

There is no choice, he said months later in the hospital, a new resolve tightening his arms as he gripped her. Down the hall their baby slept, swaddled in white cloth.

> *"I stay close to Nastya,*
> *Clutching her sleeve,*
> *Too fearful to pick*

And too frightened to leave.

"A twig cracks—I shriek:
'Nastya, look here!'
As out of the bushes
Two faces appear."

That summer, Vassily was called upon to read from his new collection of children's verse to crowds at parks and Pioneer camps. Until repetition glazed into soothing numbness, Nina seethed when she heard Vassily recite this poem. She hated him then, hated the carefree parents and their healthy children. She must hate him still, or why would she torture him this way? Because the nightmares he rode out for years—thrashing, grimacing even in sleep from the effort not to cry out—were never enough for her. In Nina's own dreams she glimpses their daughter on crowded streets. Always Dasha is exactly the age she should be, a tall redhead now, preoccupied, rooting through her purse or talking into a telephone, oblivious to her mother's voice.

"It's only our neighbors,
Kolya and Serge,
Serge covered in red
From his chin to his ears."

As the chirrups grow boisterous, a woman's voice bleeds thinly from the crowd, synchronized with Vassily's. For a moment Nina thinks she herself—the ghost of her young, expectant self—has begun to recite, her voice ricocheting across the tunnel by some acoustic trick.

"That's it!" Vassily shouts.

They all crane their necks, seeking out the source of the calm, steady alto, as faint as a radio broadcast from a distant city.

The camera's beam dashes like a searchlight across the tunnel and encircles a woman in her forties. A ring of perspiration pastes her light brown hair to her round face; her shy eyes gaze bravely forward. Nina recognizes her. Unlike the others, this one meets Nina's eyes and nods respectfully when she passes by their table. Nina has always thought her capable of kindness.

> " 'Our mama told us
> She'd make us some jam,
> But Serge is no help,'
> Says Kolya, sweet as a lamb.
>
> "Serge screws up his eyes
> And he's started to cry.
> 'It's just that they're good,
> And my throat was so dry!' "

When Vassily mimics a saucer-eyed little boy, a ruffle of laughter sweeps through the underpass. Somewhere down the line, another woman joins in.

Then another. Four, five, six—the voices braid like ribbons. The cameraman steps back, painting the soft, careworn faces with effervescent light.

> " 'Now now,' Nastya says,
> 'Enough of your tears.
> There's four of us now
> And we've nothing to fear.' "

So accustomed to chanting, the women slip one by one into the singsong rhythm and common key. All these months they have ignored Nina and Vassily. And yet, since childhood, his poem has been nestled in their memories.

> " 'Seriozha, I want you
> To look out for bears.
> And protect my sister—
> Keep them out of her hair.
>
> " 'As for you, Sissie,
> You must be wary
> And keep little Serge
> From eating the berries.' "

Bathed in shimmering whiteness, the women's faces are cameo moons. They sway as they chant, arms draped across shoulders, and strike each word with a clear, ringing tone. Vassily, bouncing in the center of the underpass, is the conductor: arms waving, lips puckering and stretching like an elastic band.

Newcomers creep into the tunnel from the stairs at each end, attracted by the chorus that must be rising onto the square. Nina spots the mustachioed butcher in his bloodsmeared smock and the waitresses from the German food trailer, fresh and lovely in pink aprons and paper caps. Many of the women join the chanting; others nod dazedly, openmouthed, as if they expect the words to spring to their lips.

> "Seriozha and I
> Obey these commands:
> He looks out for beasts
> And I guard his hands.
>
> "Kolya and Nastya,
> Lickety-split,
> Fill up four pails
> And join us where we sit."

A mother coaxes her little girl, brown hair gathered in a sprig of tulle, toward Vassily. When he places a hand on the shoulder of her yellow-dotted dress, the child relaxes against his leg. Vassily turns and raises his eyebrows at Nina. His wrinkles and jowls are erased; his blue eyes flash like crystal.

> " 'Now you see,' Kolya says,
> 'That we had such success
> When we gathered together
> And each did our best.' "

It was not only her husband and his audience Nina had despised. She hated her daughter, too, for the memory of her milk-blue eyes, which fixed on Nina from the first moment with such trust and wisdom—yes, Nina is certain that her daughter was *wise*—that she could not hope to ever forget them.

> " 'Even children,' says Nastya,
> 'Can make up a group.
> Each group's a collective,
> Each collective, a troop.' "

Nina's hand rises to her throat, for now, against her will, it is Mrs. Wolters she hates. Because she understands that if the American woman had been given a baby as placid as Nina's instead of a restless, tormented one, she never would have given her back.

> "So now you know why
> When I'm at the dacha
> I love to pick berries
> With big sister Nastya."

The packed tunnel breaks into cheers—"Hoorah! Bravo, Author!"—and Vassily struts and preens, fists clasped overhead in victory.

Nina can stand this display no longer. She pushes through the mob of women, engulfed by the riot of voices and bodies. She reaches Vassily and grabs his arm, but he doesn't notice. She tugs harder, and he turns to beam at her, his face radiant with sweat and joy.

"Vasya!" she shouts. "What are you doing?"

"Sharing my verse, Ninochka!" He motions to his adoring public.

Nina leans in close to his ear. "Vasya," she hisses. "Don't you see?"

"What, Ninochka, what?" he says, stooping toward her.

"They're laughing, Vasya."

He smiles forgivingly. "Nina, these are my readers!"

"Vasya." She tugs his sleeve again. "They're only indulging you. Don't you see? They can't be trusted."

"You don't understand," Vassily protests, but his smile has collapsed. "These are good people," he murmurs. His eyes dart toward the table, taking in his unguarded books. Steering him by the arm, Nina leads him into the throng.

"Bravo!" the women cry as they pass, thumping Vassily on the back.

Halfway to the table, the tunnel plunges into darkness. Freezing in place, Nina stifles a scream. The cameraman has extinguished his lamp, she realizes, but this knowledge does not lessen her terror. She can't see a thing; she will fall and take Vassily down with her, and they will be left to crawl through the puddles.

"Vasya!" Nina screams.

"Darling, dearest," Vassily says, loosening her fingers from his sleeve. He edges into the lead and slips her arm through his. "Follow me."

Slowly her eyes adjust; animated faces rise up from the blackness. Nina sees the reporter and cameraman pushing toward the stairs, the women waiting by the table, tattered rubles outstretched. She lets Vassily guide her into position and then tucks her hands in her pockets to hide her trembling fingers. She works to summon up her customary expression, equal parts humility and pride. Vassily withdraws his silver anniversary pen from his coat and asks the woman closest to him for her name. Out of the corner of Nina's eye, the young men ascend the steps, clapping each other on the back, the swirling fluff carrying them away, into light.

MY MOTHER'S GARDEN

Spring had come to my hometown. When I got off the bus at the entrance to the contamination zone, Oles was standing at the guard station in a lightweight uniform instead of his padded military jacket, his gun swung loosely over his back. The thaw seemed to have improved his usually sullen mood; he nodded his appreciation of the flowered fabric I'd brought for his wife and let me pass through the gate without even looking at my documents.

I strayed from the silent, wide street that led into the abandoned town, turning instead into the forest. I prefer to take the long route to my mother's house in the village, averting my eyes from the town's yawning high-rise apartment buildings, the rusting yellow Ferris wheel, and, in the far distance, the plant itself. Here the trees grew dense and undisturbed, and the scent of melted ice and new leaves filled the air. The fresh, heady smell hadn't yet reached our new home—funny that after twelve years I still think of it as "new"—less than fifty kilometers away on the barren, flat steppe.

I emerged from the woods into the broad field where I used to play as a child. During my last visit, just a month ago, it had been a smooth blanket of snow, but now feathery grass reached my knees. Across the field, the village looked almost as it did just before the evacuation, the little pastel houses rising in two neat rows, shaded by budding trees. White clouds meandered across a sky the color of periwinkles. A breeze blew up from the river, rustling the grass and swaying the sign that leaned in the middle of the field, its red warning chipped and peeling.

"Yuuuulia!" Mama cried, brandishing her ax in greeting. She and her friend Ganna, their aprons filled with pine branches, met me in the field. They smiled, wide and gap-toothed, squinting in the cool sunlight, their soft fat faces framed with kerchiefs. They were waiting for me to touch them, a kiss or a pat, but I hesitated, and the moment passed.

"Ganna, take some of these logs I've brought Mama," I said. But they had begun to divvy up their branches, each scolding the other for not taking her fair share.

Inside the house, I stacked the logs by the stove. "I've got a perfectly good forest in my backyard, and you bring me fire-wood," Mama complained.

She made me a cup of tea and examined my loot, grunting her approval at the sausage links, the bag of sugar, the box of tea. "Enough for a dress," I said, unfolding a length of flowered fabric. The white material shone like a beam of light in the run-down house, where the teacups were stained brown and wallpaper roses were buried beneath a layer of grit.

Mama showed me a bucketful of green onions she'd grown in her garden. "Delicious," she said, chomping on one. "Here, you try."

"Mama, you know I won't eat that," I said.

"Summer is coming," she said. "Ganna's Oksana is bringing her little girls here in a few weeks."

"They should be arrested for bringing children here." Each time I visit, my mother hints that she'd like me to bring my thirteen-year-old daughter, Halynka, to see her. She doesn't seem to understand that it is something I will never do.

"Look at this beautiful onion." She sliced the tip off a stalk and held it beneath my nose. It smelled sweet. Juice coated the tender white rings like syrup on a cut pine. "They come up earlier than before, and they taste better, too."

"How many times do I have to tell you, Mama? Just because it looks healthy doesn't mean it is." With the possible exception of God, my mother only believes in what she sees.

"I had a visitor the other day," she said in a singsong voice that told me she was planning to win the argument with a sneak attack. "I heard something rustling outside, and I thought it was a deer or a rabbit. I looked out the window and nearly jumped out of my skin. There was a man poking around my garden with one of those counters, wearing white clothes and a mask. He looked like a cosmonaut."

"We should all dress like that around here."

" 'What are you doing in my garden?' I shouted. He came to the door and started speaking to me in Russian."

"Who was he?"

"He told me that he was an American and he didn't speak Ukrainian."

"An American? What did he want?"

"Some of my onions. He told me he was a scientist and he wanted to do a test on them."

"Did you give him some?"

"I did, but only to teach him a lesson in hospitality. This American, he was trespassing on my property, wearing a mask, like the very air he's stealing isn't good enough for him."

"Maybe he'll come back and put some fear into you."

"There's nothing to be afraid of here." Her fingers fluttered over the fabric daisies and carnations. On the bus, I had pictured myself draping the material around her waist, taking measurements, then cutting and stitching. Mama's fingers were so stiff and callused that I doubted she could thread a needle anymore. But now I was ready to leave.

She filled one of my plastic bags with onions. "Here. These'll make Mykola strong."

"Thank you, Mama." There was no sense in refusing.

"Soon the grandchildren will be here," she said.

"You just told me that, Mama."

"Healthy, playful kids, they are. Not a one of them sick."

"For now, maybe."

"They'll eat our berries. Drink water from the well."

"Halynka's not coming here, Mama." I gave her a swift kiss, my lips glancing her cheek, my hand grazing her sweater. It never ceases to shame me, this fear I have of touching my mother, of carrying the poison in her skin and clothes to my daughter. And I could tell by her rigid posture, her refusal to yield to my touch, that Mother was ashamed of me, too, and that she had been ashamed outside when I stood stiffly in front of her and Ganna.

"Mama, would you do something for me?"

"Eh?"

"If the American comes back, see if he can stop by here next Saturday, say at two o'clock."

"I know what I'll say if he tells me he didn't like my onions: 'Go back home and eat American onions, then!' We'll see what he has to say to that."

"Just ask him, all right, Mama? I'll come back again next week."

"Don't trouble yourself. I do just fine on my own."

I walked out the front way, down the dirt road, past the tottering deserted houses of former neighbors. I was born in this village and lived here until I was twenty-three, when I moved into my husband's apartment in the nearby town. The windows of the cottages are still framed with hand-carved woodwork, but the paint is bleached and flaking, and many of the panes are broken. I usually turn away as I walk past, out of respect for those who left their homes so quickly, in such disarray. But this time as I passed the Teslenkos', I looked, just for a second. An old loom was set up in the front room, strung with gray yarn, or perhaps just cobwebs, and something pink hung out of an opened bureau drawer. Their daughter, my daughter's best friend, died six months ago. I tossed the bag of onions down on the side of the road and watched it disappear into the weeds.

At home, my husband was standing in the scruffy yard of our sinking apartment building in his tracksuit and house slippers, talking to the old women seated on the bench. He was gesturing wildly, knees bent and feet apart in an anchoring stance, as if he expected the world to take off at any moment. Mykola was once considered a handsome man—certain people were surprised he chose someone as plain as me to marry—but the neighbors do not notice his wavy hair and solid build anymore. I am grateful that we settled here with our own people after the accident, rather than among strangers in Kiev. Mykola can wobble about the yard shouting nonsense, and no one will talk about him behind his back. Here, people make allowances.

"The pistons need to be kept clean," he was saying. "It's the most important thing. The most important!" The women were nodding; like me, they have learned to pretend they understand his discourses on automobile repair. Mykola was one of the first men to participate in the cleanup at the reactor, and shortly afterward he began to suffer from dizzy spells. He was fired from his job as a mechanic five years ago, after he lost control of a car and crashed into a tree. That day marked the beginning of his confused thoughts and odd behavior.

"Be careful, I'm dirty," I said, backing away when Mykola reeled toward me.

"How's Mama?" one of the women asked about their old friend.

"As stubborn as ever," I said.

"We should all be as stubborn as her," said Evhenia Vlodimirovna. "She's living in her own home, happy as can be."

"She wants me to bring Halynka to visit her."

"Why shouldn't you?"

"Sure, why not?" echoed Maria Sergeyevna. "Not for long, of course."

Mykola picked up a candy wrapper and disappeared inside the building. I heard him shuffle up the stairs, then the whine of the garbage chute.

"I'm not taking her there," I said. "It's bad enough that I go."

"Listen to me, Yulia." Evhenia wagged her finger at me. "You know why they don't want us to move back?"

"Why?" I asked.

"It would cost too much to start up the town again after all these years. They'd have to redo the electricity and telephone lines and such. That's the only reason why. I saw it on television."

"An American scientist came by my mother's house," I said. "He's going to do a test on her onions."

"See?" Evhenia said. "He'll tell you there's nothing to worry about, and you can let your mother have a nice visit from her granddaughter before she dies."

"We'll see," I said.

Upstairs, I undressed in the bathroom, dumping everything into the bathtub, even my muddy boots. Then I turned on the shower, hot, and scrubbed my skin until it was red and raw. I lathered my hair with shampoo, stomped my clothes underfoot, and rinsed the boots, inside and out, until finally I felt clean again. Then I fetched Halynka from the Teslenkos' place, where she was watching television with Danylo, their son. Halynka left the apartment without saying good-bye, as if she were just going off to the bathroom.

"Grandmama says hello," I told her on the stairs, but she had nothing to say to that. She hasn't seen her grandmother since Mama disappeared two years ago, leaving only a note that read, "I've gone home. Come and visit me." Halynka cried for days after that. Her grandmother practically raised her; I've worked as a bookkeeper for the grocery store since we moved here twelve years ago. Halynka didn't understand when I explained that she couldn't visit her grandmother, because the village would make her sick. After a while Halynka simply stopped asking about her. I suspect she feels abandoned by her grandmother, though she has never said this to me directly.

Halynka does not like to reveal herself to me. I began to notice this fact a year ago, when the Teslenkos' daughter was diagnosed with thyroid cancer. During the next six months Halynka often slept on the floor next to Viktoria's bed and even traveled with the family to the hospital in Kiev. Lilia, Viktoria's mother, told me that Halynka would rub her friend's back for hours to help ease the terrible pain. In the months since Viktoria's death, Halynka has spent most of her time outside of school with the Teslenkos, returning home only to sleep and eat. She has developed an attachment to Lilia that I envy, and a closeness to sixteen-year-old Danylo that worries me.

We cooked supper in silence, cutlets and fried potatoes. When the food was almost done, Halynka went to the balcony to call in her father, but he wasn't outside.

I found Mykola in the bedroom, lying in the dark. "Please," he whispered.

One of his migraines had descended, so I placed a damp towel on his forehead and shut the door. I would sleep on the couch so as not to disturb him with my snoring. I knew that the next evening I would find the apartment in perfect order, the dishes put away, my clothes ironed, the rugs vacuumed. He has grown increasingly tidy since the car crash, taking over responsibilities I assumed in the early years of our marriage. But I try not to compare our present life to the past. We are two different people now; it is the only explanation that makes sense.

Coming home from work a few days later, I found Lilia Teslenko waiting for me in the yard. She was trim in her housedress, her short, dark hair neatly curled, and she smiled at me as I approached, her hand shading her eyes. Ignoring Mykola, who was talking with his lady friends, she asked me up for tea. She had sent Danylo and Halynka off on an errand, she told me, so that we could have a nice, quiet chat.

I sat at the kitchen table, dreading whatever it was she had to say.

"I haven't taken the opportunity, Yulia, to express how grateful I am that my Viktoria had such a wonderful friend as Halynka," she said as we sipped our tea.

"Viktoria was a precious gift to Halynka," I said. "She misses her terribly."

"Yes, I know." Lilia looked into her cup. "She often talks to me, and to Danylo, about her feelings, her grief. It has been difficult for all of us."

I was silent, steeling myself.

"Yulia, I'm worried about Halynka." She met my eyes. "I feel she depends on me and Danylo too much. It's as if she expects us to be her family. As if she hopes to take over Viktoria's place in our hearts."

"I'm sure she would never expect that," I said. But in truth, I wasn't sure at all.

"Perhaps I'm overstating it. But I am worried about her, and I just don't have the energy . . ." Her hands were laced tightly on the table. "To be frank, I don't want another daughter. And Danylo doesn't want a sister, or a girlfriend—do you understand what I'm saying?"

I stood up. "I understand. I'm sorry Halynka has been such a burden."

"Oh, not a burden. Please, don't think that. But . . . I think she needs to spend more time with her family—with you, at least."

I felt a surge of protectiveness for my husband. Why were his eccentricities more shameful than Viktoria's illness, when they both flowed from the same source?

"I'll make sure she doesn't bother you anymore," I said. "You've had a difficult enough time. I should have intervened earlier."

Halynka came home an hour later and went straight to her room. Finding her lying on the bed, I sat down and squeezed her shoulder. The narrow angel wings of her back rose up in defense, and I moved my hand away.

"I had a talk with Lilia Teslenko today," I said.

"I know." Her voice was small and weary.

"I told Lilia that I wanted you to visit them less often. Your father and I hardly see you."

"I want to go stay with Grandmama for the summer," she said.

"Darling, you know I won't let you go there."

"There are some little kids who spend the whole summer with their grandparents," she said.

"Their parents are making a mistake. Those children will get sick, like Viktoria."

"I don't care if I get sick."

"Halynka, don't say that." I longed to cradle her thin body in my arms, but I thought of my own need to protect myself from my mother—an urge perhaps less warranted than my daughter's need to wall herself off from me—and I restrained myself.

"Papa wouldn't care if I went to Grandmama's," she said. "He doesn't even notice me."

"Halynka, that's not true." But in a way it was. As he slowly lost his mind, Mykola had become more and more perplexed by Halynka, avoiding her until they were like roommates in a communal apartment. "We would both miss you very much."

"I've never even seen the place where I was born," she said.

Her voice was high and slow; she was drifting off to sleep.

"It was just like any other Soviet town. There was nothing special about it." This was true, except, of course, that it had been our home. But I didn't want her to get any romantic notions about the town. I wanted her to look ahead to the future, to go to college, to move away, to Kiev or even to Europe. I wanted her to forget that she had been born in a place so elusive and unnatural that its entire population had disappeared overnight.

"Drink, drink," I heard my mother say as I approached her house the next Saturday.

A man was sitting at the kitchen table, his body covered in brilliant white, from his jumpsuit to a cloth mask that revealed only his eyes—brown, crinkled at the edges—to a stiff white cap. Mama was wafting a cup of tea under his nose. Between them lay several onion stalks, a notebook and pen, and a tape recorder, its spools turning.

"Please turn that off," I said.

"I was hoping to interview you and your mother," the man said. His Russian was purer than my own. "My name is George. George Hayes. I'm an environmental toxicologist." He rose, and I saw that he was wearing rubber gloves.

"This is Yulia, my daughter," Mama said.

I had no intention of talking to a stranger about my life, and I felt protective of my mother's privacy as well. "Please," I said. "We don't want to be recorded."

He turned off the machine, and we both sat down.

"Go on, tell her," Mama said. "Tell her what you told me about my onions."

"I ran a Geiger counter over them, and there's no question they're highly contaminated. She shouldn't be eating anything from that garden. She shouldn't drink the well water or burn wood from the forest. She shouldn't be living here at all."

"I've told her all of this a thousand times," I said.

"Tell her the rest," Mama said.

"I did some tests on these onions," the American said. "Despite the radiation, or maybe even because of it, they're quite robust. You can tell just by the size and color, but the cell structure and nutritional value are both strong as well."

"It's like I told you. They're even better than before," Mama said.

"What difference does it make if they're going to make her sick?" I said.

"Well, yes, exactly. There's no doubt they're inedible," he said.

"He says it's healthy," Mama said.

"Not healthy, exactly . . . Let me explain. I've been testing mice in the area, and I've found that they're actually becoming bigger and stronger with each generation." He spoke quickly, with increasing fervor. "All over the zone, I'm finding these amazing examples of nature's ability to preserve itself, and even to advance genetically. But the acceleration we see in these onions—and that I've noticed in my mice—is abnormal. It may lead to mutations as the years go by."

"I'll give you some tomatoes when they're ready, and potatoes in the fall," Mama said. "Real beauties. I'll make you some soup."

I scraped back my chair. "May I speak to you outside?"

"Of course," the scientist said.

We stood by the garden fence. "I want you to stay away from my mother," I said.

"Stay away?"

"You're confusing her, and I'm the one who has to cope with her."

"I'm sure I can make her understand—"

"She's trying to talk me into bringing my thirteen-year-old

daughter here for a visit."

"Oh, you shouldn't do that."

"Of course not. But she points to her onions, her berries, her clear water, and she tells me there can't possibly be anything wrong with them, because they look healthy and they taste good."

"But doesn't she know . . ."

"She ran away from our new home seven times in the first ten years after we moved, until she finally convinced the guard to let her back in. She's determined to die here. No, she doesn't understand. She doesn't believe that something she can't see can hurt her."

He shook his head. "I guess it would be hard to argue with that point of view."

"Her friends' grandchildren visit them every summer. The parents let their kids drink the dirty water and breathe the dirty air, and she thinks I'm unreasonable for not letting my daughter join them." I frowned at him. "The wind goes right through that mask of yours. I can see it."

He looked away. "It's better than nothing. Would you like me to bring you some gear?"

I shook my head. "I don't worry about myself."

"For your daughter's sake, you should."

I turned back toward the house.

"I won't confuse your mother anymore, I promise," he called after me. "In fact, I'll try to talk some sense into her."

"Ha!" I said over my shoulder. "I've been trying to do that for the past twelve years."

I thought I would wait another month before returning to the village. My visits seemed only to agitate my mother and myself, and I knew there was nothing I brought that she truly needed or even wanted. Her little community of elderly squatters—

there are about ten of them—gathers on Sundays at the village prayerhouse, and there is a delivery of bread twice a week. Sometimes the old men share the fish they catch in the polluted river with Mama and the other women. A doctor comes by to check on their health and distribute their pensions, and some teenage boys bring them provisions, for a fee. It is a pleasant life for my mother, and perhaps a more peaceful end than might have been predicted for a child who was born in the aftermath of the famine and grew up during the German occupation.

There was another reason I stayed away: the children would be arriving soon. I did not want to see the wistful expression on my mother's face as she fed them bread with jam made from contaminated cranberries. I did not want to see them playing in the sun, their little bodies soaking up the poison that was resting in my own daughter's body, waiting to attack.

For the next two weeks, life seemed to be getting back to normal. Halynka began to come home straight from school and study with her bedroom door ajar, music playing softly. She told me shyly one day that she was going to be presented with an award for her high marks. I watched her walk across the school stage, fresh and pretty in her pale blue dress, a matching ribbon trailing in her shiny brown hair. There was a moment of silence for the three students who had died in the past year—Viktoria and two others. Lilia Teslenko approached us afterward, her eyes brimming with tears, Danylo at her side. I'm ashamed to say that I felt a certain satisfaction when Halynka pulled away from the woman's embrace.

On the first day of summer vacation, Halynka was gone when I returned from work. When she still hadn't come home by the time supper was ready, I called down to Mykola and the old women from the balcony. "I saw her walk off this morning, and I haven't seen her since," Evhenia Vlodimirovna yelled. Mykola only gazed at me blankly. I went to the Teslenkos', and

Lilia woke Danylo from a nap, but he said he hadn't seen Ha-lynka all day.

Mykola was agitated during supper, giving me a long lecture on carburetors and crankshafts. While I cleaned up the kitchen, he pulled the chairs away from the table and ran his homemade vacuum over the rug again and again. I looked up from the dishes and was startled to see a man standing in the hallway, dressed in tan pants and a blue pullover shirt. As I moved toward Mykola to snap off the machine, I realized it was the American scientist, stripped of his protective clothing.

"I'm sorry—I knocked, but there was no answer," he said. He was balding, and his face was round, childlike, though he was at least forty.

"Pleased to make your acquaintance," Mykola said when I introduced them. Sometimes strangers provoke him to emerge momentarily from his little world.

"I was just at the entrance of the zone," the American said. "Your daughter's there."

"What?" I cried. "Where is she now?"

"The guard is holding her there. She said she wanted to see her grandmother, but he wouldn't let her in. Did you tell her that she could go there?"

"No, no, of course not."

"Have you come from Moscow?" Mykola asked. "Have you come for the cleanup?"

"The cleanup?"

"George is American, Mykola," I said. "He's a scientist."

"Your daughter wouldn't let me drive her home. Can I take you there?"

"I would be so grateful if you would," I said, grabbing my purse. "Mykola, I'll be home soon with Halynka."

The American drove an old Lada that stalled frequently as we drove along the wide dark road toward the town. George told me that he was a professor back in Boston but had studied in Moscow when he was young and returned there often to work with Russian scientists. He had been living here in Ukraine for a couple of months, renting an apartment in New Martinovichi and going into the zone every day to collect samples for his experiments.

"Your family back in America must miss you," I said.

"Well, I'm divorced, and I don't have any children. But I suppose my parents miss me."

"I'm sure they're proud of the work you do."

"They don't understand what I do." He smiled at me. "Just like your mother. I've been talking to her, by the way. I've been trying to convince her that it would be dangerous for your daughter to visit her."

"I appreciate that, but I think you're wasting your time. She's a stubborn old woman. Unfortunately, as you've found out, my daughter takes after her."

The border crossing was a circle of light surrounded on all sides by darkness, the tall abandoned buildings of the town rising like black monoliths in the distance. Halynka was sitting inside the little guard station with Oles, drinking tea.

"Halynka," I said. "Your father and I were worried sick about you."

"I was going to visit Grandmama." I noticed a duffel bag by her chair, packed full.

"I told her she couldn't go anywhere without her parents' permission," Oles said.

"Thank you, Oles. Halynka knew she was forbidden to come here." I tugged her roughly by the arm. "Hurry up. We've taken enough of Mr. Hayes's time already."

We rode back in silence, save for the rattling of the car and its tendency to putter to a stop every few kilometers. Halynka sat in the backseat and stared out the window. For a moment I imagined we were an American family on vacation, driving through Colorado or California, looking for a hotel where we could spend the night. It was a silly fantasy, and not one I wished would come true. Americans had their own problems, after all. George had had a wife and somehow failed to keep her. My husband and I loved each other in our peculiar way, and our precious daughter was healthy and safe.

Back at home, I thanked George for his help and followed Halynka up to her bedroom. She was pulling clothes out of her bag, not looking at me.

"You know, your grandmother could have stayed here, but she didn't," I said. "She decided to leave us."

Halynka looked at me with tears in her eyes. "Does she know about Vika?"

"Yes, darling, I told her. But she doesn't understand what made Viktoria sick."

"Maybe she's right. Maybe it wasn't the town. Maybe Vika got sick for no reason."

"It's possible, sweetheart, but you know what the doctors said."

"I was going to talk to Grandmama about her."

"You could write a letter, and I could take it to her. Would you like that?"

"I don't want to write her a letter. I want to talk to her."

"I wish I could let you, darling. Would you like to talk to me instead?"

She shook her head.

I left her room and went out on the balcony. Down below, Mykola was bent over the American's car, his hands darting like a pianist's under the hood. George shone a flashlight and handed tools to Mykola. The old women watched from their bench. The windows of the other buildings in the settlement were lit up, gold and flickering blue boxes. Children were playing ball off on the horizon, barely visible against the black sky and black earth, their cries punctuating the still air. Men gathered at the car, shaking George's hand, and Mykola began to narrate his gestures for the benefit of the crowd. A man lit a cigarette for George. Slender plumes of smoke drifted in the dim light, disappearing into the blackness.

Two little blond girls in summer dresses were playing in the sunlit field when I emerged from the pine forest the following Saturday. One dropped, disappearing into the tall grass, and then the other stumbled about with her eyes closed until she tripped over her friend. When I approached, they stared at me, still as statues, waiting until I had crossed the field before continuing their game.

My mother met me at the door. She had made a dress from the fabric I'd brought; the carnations and daisies widened across her broad belly. "What do you have?" she asked, grabbing my bags.

"Aren't you even going to say hello?" I asked.

She pushed past me. "Tara, Olya, come here!" The little girls ran up to her from the field. "Girls, take these things to Grandmama, and tell her this is what you're to eat. All right?" The girls looked into the bags at the flour and salt, the sticks of wood, and nodded solemnly. "Go on home, now."

"What was that all about?" I asked.

"Ganna doesn't feed them right," Mama said, settling heavily into her chair.

"Oh?"

"That American's been coming around, talking to us, taking pictures."

"Has he?" I wondered if he had told Mama about Halynka's attempt to visit her, and I decided he was probably more discreet than that.

"Here, I want you to see this." She picked up a photograph from the table. Her face was in the center of the picture, unsmiling, determined. "He gave this to me yesterday." The photo was printed on thick paper in tones of green, and the image was strewn with faint white dots. "See the snow?" she said. "The American said it's radiation. He said he has a special camera that can see it."

I stared in fascination at the photograph. It did look as if snow were falling inside the house, swirling around my mother, speckling her face.

"Yulia, do you think the American is an honest man?" Mama asked as she fiddled with a handkerchief.

I put the photograph aside. "Yes, Mama. I do think he's an honest man."

She stood up. "I don't want you to come here anymore."

"Why not, Mama?"

"I should never have told you to visit." Her voice quavered, and she brushed her eyes with the back of her hand.

"Mama." I reached for her, but she pushed me away.

"The American and I showed the picture to Ganna, but she just laughed. Stupid old fool. That's what we all are—stupid old fools."

"The girls will be all right," I said. "They'll go home soon."

Mama cupped her face in her hands. "Halynka was outside the entire day after the accident."

"Shh, shh, Mama." I held her shoulders, trying to draw her near, but she shrugged me away. "Halynka's all right," I said. "She's healthy."

"She used to have such a terrible cough, it would keep her awake at night."

"She hasn't had it for a long time."

"Her little friend died, the blond girl. They were the same age." She crumpled against me, sobbing.

All this time, she had only needed to see it with her own eyes. I held her tight, wanting to both shake her and kiss her.

I took the picture home. "Come with me," I said to Mykola, and he followed me up to the apartment. Halynka watched in surprise as I turned off the television and placed the photograph on the coffee table. "You wanted to see your grandmother," I said. "I brought you a picture of her. Don't touch it—it's dirty. But I want you to look at it, closely." Then I went into the bathroom to cleanse myself.

When I came out in my robe, Mykola and Halynka were facing each other on the couch. "They gave us two counters to keep track of the levels, one in your boot, the other in your pocket," Mykola said, slapping his chest. He jumped to his feet. "Into the uniform. Heavy aprons lined with lead. Gloves. A big mask." He pantomimed pulling on the uniform. "Then up to the roof of the reactor. Five minutes at a time, that's all we had." He pushed an imaginary shovel against the carpet. "Quick, quick, push through the rubble, look for the rods. Watch your step. Helicopters loud overhead." He whirled around, staring at the ground. "Here's some." He made a scooping motion. "Collect as much as you can. Dark rods. Find the trash bin. Careful—it'll burn through your boots. Hard to see. Time's running out. Hurry up." He dashed around the living room, staring intently at the ground. "Ah, here's one. And here's some more. They're calling now; time's up." He tossed the shovel aside. "They grab the counters, no chance to read them." He collapsed into a chair, panting. "Time for a smoke."

I stood at the edge of the room, watching as Halynka helped Mykola light a cigarette. "Good job, Papa," she said softly, and retreated to the couch.

Mykola wiped sweat from his forehead as he puffed smoke into the room. "Just enough time for a smoke. Then up to the roof. Up to the roof again."

When I came home from work on Monday, Halynka was lying on the couch reading, and there was a stack of library books on the floor beside her. For a moment I was hopeful she would spend the summer absorbed in literature, but when I flipped through some of the books, I saw that she was reading about the accident. The writing was dense and technical, illustrated with complicated graphs. When I asked if she found the books interesting, she only shrugged.

The next evening after supper we took the bus to New Martinovichi. The American answered his door wearing his casual clothes. "Yulia," he said. "And Halynka. Please come in."

"I'm sorry to stop by unannounced," I said. "I got your address from Oles."

"I'm glad you're here."

"Halynka has some questions she'd like to ask you." The apartment was terribly messy. Papers were strewn about the tables and floor, and there were half-filled cups of coffee everywhere.

"Of course." George cleared a space on the kitchen table, and he and Halynka sat down.

I moved about the apartment, gathering the dirty dishes, and washed them slowly. I heard my daughter's shy voice gaining confidence as she asked the American about safety procedures at the reactor and the odds of a meltdown happening again. George answered her questions directly and thoroughly, using simple terms. I could tell he was being careful not to frighten her, yet he expressed concern about the damage caused by the accident and the possibility that someday it could happen again, here or in another part of the world.

I served them tea and sat quietly at the other end of the table.

"Were you alive when it happened, Halynka?" George asked when she had run out of questions.

Halynka looked at me. "I had just had my first birthday. Right, Mama?"

"Yes. We had a party the day after the accident. Before we knew anything was wrong."

"No one had any idea, did they?" George asked.

I shook my head. "They waited two days to evacuate us." I felt my throat tightening.

"Were you scared?" Halynka asked.

"Not scared . . . It's hard to describe." They both looked at me, waiting. "We should be going," I said, standing up.

George insisted on driving us home. The car ran smoothly, and he praised my husband's repair job. In front of our building, Mykola ran up and opened Halynka's door, then mine. He greeted the American and trotted off.

"Wait, Papa," Halynka called after him.

"Thank you for talking to her," I said to George.

"I can only tell her the facts. She'll have to find out the rest from you."

His tape recorder was lying on the seat between us. "Could I borrow this?" I asked.

"Sure. I won't need it anymore." George told me that he was returning to America in a few days but that he hoped to see me next summer. Before I got out of the car, he showed me how to use the machine, testing it on his own voice. As I climbed the stairs behind my husband and daughter, I imagined George walking into his empty, quiet apartment in Boston. Entering my own home, I smiled, for it occurred to me that he was probably feeling sorry for me as he drove away.

"Halynka?" my mother shouted. "This is Grandmama."

"You don't need to talk so loud, Mama," I whispered. We were sitting at her kitchen table, and I was holding the tape recorder up to her mouth.

"Halynka, this is Grandmama talking to you on the machine," she shouted. "Your mama said you'll be able to hear me. I want to say hello to you. I hope you're doing well. Everything's fine here. My tomatoes are growing. The flowers are blooming." She paused and looked out the window, breathing loudly through her nose. "I heard about Viktoria. I'm so sorry, my dear." She looked at me.

"You can stop if you like."

She turned back to the machine and cleared her throat. "I told your mama that she wasn't allowed to visit me anymore, but she came anyway. She said you can talk back to me on the machine if you want. I would like that very much. I miss you terribly, my darling."

When we had finished, I walked down the road in front of the house. Reaching the main street, I turned toward the town rather than heading back toward the border. I held the tape recorder to my mouth and began to speak.

"Halynka, I'm walking into your hometown. Since I won't let you come here, I thought I would describe it for you. I myself haven't been here since we left. I was afraid to come here, to see our old home looking so empty and desolate.

"The reactor is off in the distance, towering over the town. There are two great smokestacks, striped, and huge buildings shaped like a mountain. From here it all looks normal. This was a young city, built for workers in the plant. So many of us were just starting our families, and there were lots of children here. I'm passing some apartment buildings now. It almost seems as if they're not empty at all. There are curtains on the windows, and I can see furniture inside.

"Here's a store where I used to shop. I brought you with me, of course." I looked through the window. "There are still cans of food on the shelves. I recognize the old paper labels.

"I'm turning onto the street where we used to live." I heard some birds chirping, but that was all. "I can see the Ferris wheel between some buildings. It was brought in especially for May Day. Your papa and I had planned to take you to the carnival. But of course we all left just a few days before.

"Here it is, our building." My voice caught, and I lowered the recorder from my mouth. I stared up at the window, waiting until my breathing was even. "It's just six stories high, and we were on the top floor. It looks like the pink curtains I sewed have faded. We left the apartment neat as a pin. Your father used to tease me about the way I tidied up before we went anywhere. I swept and did the dishes that day, even though we only had a few hours to get ready."

I peered through a scratched plastic window. "The entryway is dark and dingy, paper and garbage everywhere. We stood there waiting for the buses—by that time we knew better than to stand outside. It was hot and crowded, and you cried."

I had planned to go upstairs, look for the spare key under the doormat, enter our home, and describe it for Halynka. But now that I was here, I was frightened. The apartment might have been looted; at the very least it would be dusty and terribly quiet. I turned back to the road, knowing that I had come as close as I could.

"The accident happened in the middle of the night, as George told you. In the morning there was a steady dark line of smoke coming out of the reactor. Your papa told me he had heard an explosion. I had slept through it. We turned on the radio, but nothing was said about it on the news.

"Of course we didn't have time to think about the reactor. It was an important day: your first birthday party. I put on my nicest dress, and your papa wore a suit and tie. I had sewn you a yellow dress edged with lace.

"We walked over to the park around noon. I'm heading there now. It was a warm spring day, and everyone was outside. Women were shopping at the market, and children were playing. There was no sign that anything was wrong. Here, here is the park. Back then the grass was worn away, but now it's overgrown with weeds.

"Your uncle Ivanko butchered a pig the week before, and my friends and I prepared sausages, dumplings, and meat pies. Your grandmama made pancakes, and Lilia Teslenko baked a four-layer frosted torte. We had gone to little Viktoria's birthday celebration just a month before at their home in the village. Lilia was a great beauty, and when we were growing up, I used to be jealous of her. But after we both had baby girls, we became friendly. You and Viktoria took to each other immediately. Even when you were just a few months old, you seemed to have your own private language, cooing and laughing together.

"All of our friends were at the party. Most of them worked at the reactor, like your papa. There was talk of the explosion, and we watched the dark smoke rising into the sky. Someone said that foamy water had been gushing onto their street and that children were playing in it. But no one was really worried. You have to understand, we never imagined that anything bad would happen to us, and we were sure we would be notified if there was any reason to be concerned. But I still feel guilty for taking you outside that day. Sometimes I wonder if I would have been more sensible if I hadn't been distracted by the party. Maybe we would have all stayed inside with our windows closed. Sometimes I wonder if Lilia blames me for this.

"In the late afternoon we woke you up for the ceremony— your first haircut. Your papa stood you on a chair at the head of the table, and everyone gathered around. Your grandmother took up the scissors and snipped off a lock from your forehead. She did the same at the back of your head and then on each side, so that she had cut from north, south, east, and west, the four directions of the world. Next she passed the scissors to your uncle Ivanko, and it was his turn. Then Lilia and Yuri Teslenko cut your hair.

"You were always a good baby, rarely fussing, but on that day you were especially quiet and still, as if you realized something important was happening—almost, I thought later, as if you knew that everything was about to change. To me, your haircut was a reminder that you would grow up and leave me, just as I had left my own mother. I got a little teary, and your papa hugged me, and everyone laughed, understanding why I was sad."

I began to walk back toward the border. I was ready to see the look on Halynka's face when she heard her grandmother's voice. And I confess, I was eager for my daughter to hear my own story for the first time.

"The evacuation began the next day. They told us that we would be able to come home in three days. The envelope with your locks of hair was the only memento I packed when we left. I suppose part of me realized that we might never return, though I don't remember thinking this at the time. I threw the envelope away later, crying as I did. I threw away everything we had brought with us from the town. Of course, you didn't understand when I tried to explain that I had thrown out your favorite doll because it was dirty. How cruel I seemed to you. Do you understand now, Halynka? I didn't feel I had a choice. I had to get rid of everything from the past."

I turned off the recorder. The bus was pulling up to the gates, and Oles waved and shouted at me to hurry. I began to jog, laughing at the spectacle I was making, a middle-aged woman running to catch a bus, as if in my rush to leave the town, I had forgotten myself, just for a moment, and thought that I was still a young girl.

KITCHEN FRIENDS

On a high-ozone morning in Moscow, midsummer 1996, Leslie stood among a clutch of Russians at the corner of Prospect Mira and Novoalekseevskaya Street, squinting dreamily at the sky-blue number 48 trolleybus that was slowly rumbling toward them through the haze. Past the bus, the broad avenue sloped gently upward, disappearing into the oversized kitsch and clutter of the All-Russia Exhibition of Economic Achievements. Leslie could make out the upper loop of the gigantic Ferris wheel, the menacing hook of the sickle brandished by the enormous steel collective-farm girl, and the rocket at the top of the Sputnik Obelisk, blasting perpetually into space on a titanium trail.

The next moment, Leslie was lying flat on the sidewalk amid an explosion so loud it seemed to come from everywhere. Suddenly conscious of the shape of the earth and of her body riding it like the pointer of a compass, she clawed the pavement, certain that if she released her grip, she would tumble into the stratosphere. The blast bore down upon her, and all she could think was that gravity had been sucked up by a black hole that had spun, tornado-like, too close to earth.

Other people were scattered about the street, while some wobbled on their feet, perilously vertical. As the boom began to subside, Leslie was aware of matched tangs of pressure just inside her ears. The air was pungent with the scent of fire-works. She could make out screams and shouts, horns and car alarms, squealing brakes, but the noises were far away, tweeting and delicate.

Words hurtled through Leslie's mind and gathered into thoughts. Her theory about the disappearance of gravity was replaced with the suspicion that a bomb had exploded nearby. This suspicion was given credence when a man shouted:

"Bomba!"

Leslie lifted her head slightly. The man pointed north. She followed an imaginary string from his fingertip into a cloud of black smoke billowing from the trolleybus that a few moments before had been clattering toward the corner where she now lay.

All around Leslie, people began to lurch up from the earth, arms spread wide, like children imitating flowers in a school play. Wait for me, Leslie thought. Surveying her arms and legs, she found her limbs intact. Slowly she rose, a tender shoot blossoming to full height. Pulling loose from the street, she faced the bus and took her first steps on this new, wondrous earth.

Smoke-charred passengers clambered from the rear of the bus, arms flapping wildly. As they staggered away, cleaner passersby and would-be riders descended upon them. A young man in a red-checked blazer chased a woman with charcoal handprints on her face, her skirt ripped to her waist. Only a few people lay bleeding on the ground, tended by police. Several women sat weeping on the curb, rubbing their eyes with dirty knuckles, while others muttered to themselves and wandered close to the traffic. Men took off their soiled shirts and strutted around the crumpled carcass of the trolleybus, gesturing and pointing.

Leslie draped her arm around one of the wandering women

and told her not to worry. "I can't hear! I've gone deaf!" the woman shouted. An officer hailing passing cars guided Leslie and the woman into the backseat of a red Zhiguli driven by a small man with narrow eyes. The driver swerved madly, his rear end bobbing above the seat like a jockey's, his blaring horn a fly diving in and out of Leslie's ear. The woman gripped Leslie's hand. She looked familiar beneath the ash that veiled her flesh: middle-aged, plump, with brown-rooted orange hair—the liquor saleswoman at Produkti, the local state grocery store. Leslie, who only drank socially, had never spoken to her before.

Just a day earlier, Leslie remembered, several people had been injured in another bombing of a Moscow trolleybus. A passenger had brought an unattended bag of potatoes to the driver seconds before the device hidden inside exploded. No one had claimed responsibility, but government officials blamed Chechen rebels. Russia's war against Chechen independence, put on hold during the Yeltsin reelection blitz, was raging again.

Leslie thought of her Russian grandfather, Grandpa Serge, dead now for almost a year. What would he think if he could see her, speeding away from a terrorist attack in a gypsy cab, rubbing the arm of a shell-shocked saleswoman? A Simonov, surrounded by commoners, on the run again in their native land! He would be appalled. Leslie relaxed against the seat, her alarm settling into a pleasant buzz of alertness.

She had lived in Moscow for four years, but Leslie's Russian odyssey began in childhood. Every summer her parents, each thrice divorced by her sixteenth birthday, would chuck their only child off to her émigré grandfather's estate in Malibu. Day after day, as Grandpa Serge worked on his tan, Leslie had lain on a deck chair beside him, listening groggily to his lectures about the Simonovs' proud heritage and noble blood, which he authenticated by citing the flaws of other Russian aristocrats. "The Sheremetevs? Nothing but lackeys," Grandpa Serge snorted, as if eleven-year-old Leslie—sprawled in a two-piece swimsuit, sucking compote cocktail through a twisty straw—had argued otherwise. "The Nabokovs were poseurs, every last one!" Her parents' stormy loving and leaving made Leslie feel disposable. From Grandpa Serge she learned of a better class of Simonov, those who banded together against the whims and indignities of the outside world. Her grandfather's virulent strain of Russian seeped into her brain and clung there stubbornly, fending off the timorous advances of Wisconsin middle-school French. In her twenties, Leslie established an identity as a true Russophile, known for her love of Tolstoy, her painstaking dissections of glasnost and perestroika, and the dramatically patterned shawls she wore through Milwaukee winters.

In 1992 Grandpa Serge urged Leslie to travel to Moscow to research a book that would educate the newly uncloistered citizenry about their most important displaced family. Leslie seized on the plan. She imagined herself a minor celebrity, admired for her charming blend of Russian pedigree and American free spirit. But when she arrived in Moscow and began poring over historical documents in the state archives, her exhilaration dissolved. Her ancestors had been not benevolent patrons, but barons of the most nefarious kind—thieves, murderers, and tax cheats. In the mid–nineteenth century they had even rounded up a rogue army of their own peasants and launched a mini-revolt against the abolition of serfdom.

Visiting the family estate, Leslie found that the main house had long ago been converted into a sock factory. She was invited back for a privatization ceremony in which Moscow Light Industrial Manufacturing Plant #53 was renamed the Black Cat Joint-Stock Company. Addressing the Black Cat employees from the porch of the main house, Leslie spoke of "the importance of a truly *benevolent* leadership." As a token acknowledgment of the plant's history, the director presented her with one hundred dollars' worth of stock and ten pairs of glittering caramel-colored panty hose. The ceremony was the only bright spot in Leslie's research.

"Traitors!" Grandpa Serge raged from his deck chair that summer, shaking a pair of Black Cat panty hose in the air. The lenses of his sunglasses reflected Leslie's face back to herself—stricken twins. "A mockery! A mockery of our family honor!"

Leslie remembered how the workers, swapping whispers and cigarettes on the factory lawn, had transmogrified before her eyes into their forebears, lugging sacks of grain and leaning on wooden rakes. Dizzy with shame, she had doubled over the pool and vomited.

Back in Moscow in the fall, Leslie confided to her diary her horror over her family's crimes and her disillusionment with her grandfather, whose sense of noblesse oblige had proved as infectious as his native tongue. When she finished her outpouring, she realized that she had composed the type of slice-of-life-in-Russia columns that expatriates published week after week for other expatriates. She abandoned her book project and found an unpaid position as a columnist with the *Moscow Sparrow*, the third-largest English-language newspaper in the city. Supported by the allowance Grandpa Serge's accountant wired each month, Leslie told her story alongside the *Sparrow's* wire stories and advertorials: an American discovering her homeland, befriending the descendants of those her ancestors had enslaved. She wrote of the famous hospitality of Russians and their willingness to speak *po dusham*—from the soul—with near strangers.

By the time her grandfather died, of malignant melanoma, Leslie viewed her use of her trust fund as a subversive act. When the trolleybus bomb exploded, she had been heading to the newspaper office to deliver a column urging her readers to get to know their Russian neighbors and co-workers, her favorite theme.

At the hospital, Leslie was released within an hour by a doctor who assured her that the ringing in her ears was a sign of healing. She found her traveling companion propped up in a bed in the emergency ward, still in her tattered street clothes, but her face had been washed, and her expression of horror had calcified into grim resignation. Two doe-eyed young women in tank tops and miniskirts perched on each side of the bed, stroking the woman's arm and gazing at the tiny television at the foot of the bed.

"That's the foreigner who rescued me!" the woman shouted, pointing at Leslie.

The young women gasped and ushered Leslie onto the bed. Larisa Mikhailovna introduced herself and her daughters, Ksenia and Irina. Hearing loss, Irina told Leslie, was their mother's only symptom as well.

While the daughters cooed over her, Leslie explained that although it was true she was technically a foreigner, she was more than just an American abroad, more than just half Russian. "I'm an ordinary citizen, like you."

"Of course, of course, you're Russian, too . . . in a manner of speaking." Larisa Mikhailovna's face clouded, then cleared. "At least, you're not one of them."

"What do you mean, Larisa Mikhailovna?" Leslie said.

"Call me Lara." The woman elaborated. "I mean to say, you're not a terrorist." Lara squinted at Leslie. "Right?"

"Of course not!" Leslie cried. "Do you . . . Do you think the Chechens are responsible?"

"Who else?" scoffed Ksenia, the elder daughter.

Though Leslie hated to jump to conclusions, she had to admit that Chechen separatists were the most likely culprits.

"A survivor knows," Lara said. "Just think of how we were tossed out of our seats like popcorn. How we fought to breathe."

"I wasn't actually on the bus," Leslie confessed.

"But you *almost* were," Lara said. Leslie was riveted by the intensity of her new friend's gaze. Lara's eyes were wide set, and one of them was a lighter brown than the other, giving Leslie the sensation that the eyes belonged to two different women whose faces had swum together, as in a film dissolve. "And then you saved me!" Lara shouted.

"Well . . ." Leslie said.

"It's true! You stepped in when my own daughters couldn't. You're almost like family."

"Family?" Leslie echoed.

Lara, Ksenia, and Irina nodded, and slowly Leslie also began to nod. She relaxed against the rough sheet. Together the four of them stared at the lanky, colorfully dressed host of *Name that Tune*, bouncing from one edge of the television screen to the other like a metronome. Lara sang along with the orchestra's snippets of Russian folk songs in a high, quavering voice. Leslie sighed as the daughters stroked her arms with fingers smooth as satin. It had been so long since she touched someone, since someone touched her; even in the stores, money was passed back and forth on a dish.

Leslie had expected to accumulate a host of Russian friends in the course of her daily life, as she expected the love of a sensitive and passionate Russian man and two well-behaved Russian children. These riches eluded her. When she reported in her columns the wry truisms of her *kukhonnie druz'ya*—her kitchen friends—she might be quoting the overheard small talk of a neighbor or the girl who sold her bread. Over the years, a number of Russian men had written to express their admiration for Leslie's beauty (a fuzzy, unflattering head shot ran beside her column). They tended to propose marriage on the first date, and when Leslie demurred, they fell into sulky silence and let her pick up the check. The men had formed a composite in her memory: balding, with a brown mustache and sad, droopy eyes. Leslie was thirty-five now; was it time to cut her losses and go home? Very few people would even note her departure from Russia—perhaps as few as would mark her return to America. She couldn't help but wonder if today she had been given a reprieve.

A nurse burst through the curtain brandishing a rubber-headed hammer and shooed the visitors from the bed. Before Leslie left, Lara asked her what she did for a living.

"I'm a writer," Leslie said.

"Then you must write about this," the woman bellowed.

"This week I will not be writing about a visit to a new super-market, or to Pasternak's grave, or to the animal marketplace," Leslie scrawled in her notebook as she rode the subway home. (Though she could afford to take cabs, she wanted to face the same risks as the rest of the population.) "Today I witnessed something that altered my life in a way I do not yet understand. Today I witnessed the explosion of a bomb on a Moscow trol-leybus."

Leslie hesitated. Numerous monumental events had taken place during her years in Russia: the failed Communist putsch of 1993, the first "democratic election" earlier in the month, and the Chechen conflict, that endless bout of Whack-a-Mole. Other Western columnists called on the Russian government to reduce the indiscriminate killing of Chechen civilians and to allow the republic some degree of self-determination, but Leslie had avoided writing about the war, reluctant to tell Russians what to do. She had allowed turmoil and controversy to skirt her quiet life, but the bomb had changed that, as surely as if it had been meant for her. "The contrast between the cow-ardly terrorists," she wrote, "united by their bloodlust, and their victims, isolated and suffering in hospitals across the capi-tal, is striking."

The sky above Prospect Mira was a dingy white that might be peeled away in layers, like ancient insulation batting, to expose a bruised and angry sun. The ruined trolleybus attracted Leslie like a magnet. The mayor of Moscow, a round little man with rolled-up shirtsleeves, was surveying the damage. "We're witnessing a pattern of terrorist acts," he informed the reporters who encircled him. Workers in orange vests swept up broken glass and scraps of twisted metal. A Fuji advertisement still clung to the rear panel of the bus, but its right front side lolled on the sidewalk like an abandoned larval skin. Beyond the shattered windows, lamps twirled from the ceiling, flying saucer models. "We're going to have to do something about the Chechen diaspora," the mayor said as Leslie scuttled away, spooked by the wreckage, its contrast to her own unbroken flesh.

That night, on the TV news, Leslie spied herself and Larisa Mikhailovna ducking into the Zhiguli like hounded celebrities. Witnessing the birth of their friendship, tears sprang to Leslie's eyes. No one had died in the explosion, the anchor reported, but two passengers were hospitalized in serious condition; many of the remaining twenty-six had suffered sprains and hearing loss. The authorities were investigating bomb threats and called on citizens to report unattended packages in public places. The mayor ordered police to check the documents of anyone suspicious-looking—the same Arab-featured men they always stopped, Leslie supposed—and President Yeltsin declared Moscow "infested with terrorists." Meanwhile, Russian artillery and helicopter gunships bombarded villages in southern Chechnya.

In bed that night, jerking from the edge of sleep, Leslie relived the terror of dislocation, of being ripped from time and space. She pictured the felled trolleybus's live wire snaking down Prospect Mira, the electricity jolting the bomb's victims upright one by one. Together but apart, they were each battling this first, sleepless night. A new conviction surged through Leslie: by reaching out to these troubled souls, she could begin to make amends for the wrongs her ancestors had inflicted on their peasant predecessors. And in the process of absolving her guilt, she thought as she slid into a leaden, dreamless sleep, she might discover the close-knit circle of family and friends she had never had. She might even discover a reason to stay.

The next day at the *Sparrow* office, Jason, Leslie's editor, a twenty-two-year-old from Florida, frowned as he leafed through the twelve pages she had written on the explosion. But when Leslie showed him that the column was organized into sections of similar length, he agreed to publish it as a three-day series.

That afternoon, Leslie visited Larisa Mikhailovna's high-rise, near the exhibition center. Ksenia and Irina pulled her into the apartment, which trapped the heat of the steamy day. They had incredible news. The city had promised their mother one thousand dollars as compensation for her pain and suffering. And thanks to a hearing apparatus on loan from the hospital, she could hear much better and no longer needed to shout.

In the kitchen, Lara was pointing at the television screen, mouth agape. A slender beige cord draped from her bulbous hearing aid, which was squealing like a teakettle. On TV, a bearded man wearing black sunglasses, a beret, and military garb was speaking calmly to the camera, his fingers laced on a cloth-covered table, a pitcher of ice water at his side.

"It's S.R.!" Lara said, identifying a Chechen military commander. "He came back to life!"

He was one of the most extreme rebel leaders, Irina explained. A few months ago the government reported that S.R. had been killed, but as it turned out, he only lost an eye. He had sneaked off to Germany and disguised himself with plastic surgery.

"His friends staged the trolleybus explosions in honor of his return to Chechnya," said Lara, her voice oozing disgust. She dislodged the hearing aid and rapped it on the kitchen table. The squealing tapered off, and she shoved it back into her ear. "Didn't we tell you it was them?"

They had. How naïve Leslie must seem!

On the screen, rusted cars and trucks stacked high with furniture and bundles crept across a muddy field. Two old men trudged along on foot. A little girl stared through a car window jagged with broken glass.

"Just look at those beards, that dirty skin," said Lara.

What did Lara mean by dirty skin? Leslie wondered uneasily.

"Most foreigners don't understand." Lara patted Leslie's hand. "But you're not like them, are you?"

"No!" Leslie said. "No, I'm not!"

"Those French, those Swedes and all, the only thing they talk about is human rights." Lara's voice slid into a growl. "What about my right to ride a bus to work without being blown up?"

As the news turned to interviews with frightened Muscovites who were boycotting trolleybuses, Lara chose a bottle of wine from the carton in the kitchen—evidently a perk of her job. She began to tell Leslie about her life, speaking in a mournful voice, *po dusham,* each of her eyes staring with distinct yet equal force. She told Leslie the story of her husband's affairs, her own affair, and their subsequent divorce ten years ago. She complained about her mundane and ill-paying job as a salesclerk. Then she spoke at great length about the death of her lifelong dream of becoming an airport ground controller. Though she had graduated near the top of her class at the aviation institute, she failed the certification test because of a "mental condition" that prevented her from knowing right from left. This failure had haunted her ever since. Her daughters, silent shadows, nodded. Lara spoke late into the night, filling and refilling Leslie's glass with syrupy Moldovian wine. In great detail she described the thrill of guiding planes homeward with lighted batons. The ringing of Lara's hearing aid accompanied her somber voice like wind whistling through cracks in a wooden house, and Leslie grew woozy and limp-limbed, gazing from one to the other of the woman's mesmerizing eyes, feeling transported to the very heart of Russia.

The next morning, a photograph of S.R. covered the front page of all the newspapers. As Leslie approached the entrance to the subway, she stared at the rebel leader. He was smiling, his left hand raised in a half wave, half salute, the contours of his face hidden by his thick beard, his eyes shielded by impenetrable aviator sunglasses. Leslie bought a paper. When she returned home, she clipped the photograph, without knowing why, and tucked it in a drawer.

With another deadline approaching, Leslie wrote about the resurfacing of S.R. "It is difficult to accept that we live in a world where the followers of a Chechen commander celebrate his homecoming by bombing busloads of civilians. Russians and expatriates alike must unite against such cold-blooded evil."

In a burst of inspiration, Leslie also typed up a flyer:

Dear Prospect Mira Trolleybus Bombing Survivor:
    You have just endured a terrible ordeal and should be proud of your strength and courage. But there is no need for you to face your trauma alone. You are invited to discuss the tragedy with other victims this Friday evening at 7 p.m., Novoalekseevskaya Street, House 15,

Apartment 36.

Yours,
Leslie Simonov
The Moscow Sparrow

It took just twenty dollars to convince a local police commander to give her a list of the victims' names and addresses. Vitaly, Konstantin, Gleb, Mark—nearly half were men, Leslie noted; her heart fluttered at the prospect of seeing them with clean faces. She recruited Lara's daughters to help, and by the end of the day, they had slipped the flyer under twenty-eight apartment doors, following the route of the trolleybus north to the exhibition center and beyond, to a peaceful neighborhood where, as Ksenia pointed out, they could glimpse retired cosmonauts tending the gardens of their government-issued parcels of land.

Leslie was fortunate to live in a building that was Stalin—rather than Khrushchev—era, forged of sturdy brick and solid pipes; however, the apartments themselves were tiny. She had borrowed chairs from her downstairs neighbor, but she was unprepared when twenty-six of the twenty-eight bombing victims quietly streamed in beginning at 7:30, lining up their shoes in neat rows by the door. Now they faced her in the living room: men and women, mostly middle-aged, with a few pensioners and young people, holding cookies and sipping orange soda from paper cups. Some of them had bandages wrapped around wrists and knees; several wore hearing aids. A tall blond man with a dimpled chin stood out from the crowd. Leaning against the wardrobe, he smiled at Leslie as if they shared some private joke.

Leslie glanced at Lara, who gave a deep nod.

After thanking the survivors for coming, Leslie explained

that she herself was not on the bus when it exploded, but that the tragedy had affected her so deeply she felt as if she shared their pain. "You see, I'm an American, but I have Russian ancestors." She shook away a vision of Grandpa Serge thrashing the panty hose in the air. "I believe that as long as the terrorists are more united than we are, as long as we confront our trauma in isolation, it will be impossible for us to overcome this ordeal." Her guests nibbled their cookies with downcast eyes. "It's my privilege to give you a forum to speak to other survivors *po dusham,* tonight and in the future, with the goal of healing through conversation and friendship."

After a long stretch of silence, the tall man stepped forward. "I was wondering, that is, if it's not too crass to speak of," he said, coughing into his fist, "if anyone has gotten their compensation yet."

A murmur rose up, then subsided as a woman's voice filled the room. "I called City Hall today," she said, "and they told me that we can pick it up at the general cashier's office on the first of the month."

There was some discussion of where the cashier's office was located, and much confusion and rustling of paper as the woman repeated the address three times. Leslie began copying it onto slips of paper for those who didn't have a pencil.

"Are they giving us all the same amount?" an old man asked.

"They told me I'd get a thousand dollars," said the tall man.

Everyone agreed that they, too, had been promised a thousand dollars.

"In rubles, I suppose," a woman sniffed.

The survivors began to discuss whether they might sue for a higher figure. Some felt litigation was futile, as the government presumably had not planted the bomb, though one man advanced the theory that Yeltsin's daughter had masterminded the explosions to stir up public support for the war.

"I saw some dark-skinned types on the street after I got on at Malomoskovskaya," an old woman said. "But I don't think I could identify them now—they all look the same to me."

Another man said he'd seen S.R. bragging on the news about planting the bomb.

His followers did it, a woman corrected him.

"Leave it to the Germans to disguise one of our enemies!" an old man bellowed.

"I heard the rebels are buying their weapons from neo-Nazis in Berlin," someone said.

"Perhaps," Leslie said, raising her voice above the hubbub, "we should avoid assigning blame, and talk instead about how we might cope with the experience."

The tall man stepped forward again. "Have we decided we're satisfied with a thousand bucks each?"

The survivors looked at each other and shrugged.

"As long as they pay us," a woman said.

"I have my doubts," a man said darkly.

"Well, if it's agreed, then . . ." The tall man bowed at Leslie. "Thank you for the refreshments."

"Oh . . . you're welcome, but don't you—" Her voice was drowned out by the scraping of chair legs. "You're welcome to stay," Leslie said to several people, but they only smiled.

When the front door closed, the tall man was gone. Just five of Leslie's guests were left: Lara and her two daughters, an old woman leaning on a cane, and a man of about forty who looked like the composite of the Russian men Leslie had met through her column. He had the same drooping eyes and brown mustache, the same eyeglass case tucked in the pocket of his short-sleeved shirt, the same gray slacks and tattered brief-case. He smiled at her sadly.

Leslie looked around the room at the empty cups and cookie crumbs. It was not the wide support network she had envisioned, but perhaps a small circle of confidants would be more rewarding. Remembering the photograph of S.R. stuffed in her bureau drawer, she felt a burst of outrage, and her spirits rallied. Like the rebels, this group was small in number—but they were on the side of good, not evil.

The rebel leader began to appear in Leslie's dreams. One night he proposed marriage to her over dinner at a restaurant. When she tried to turn him down politely, he pulled a grenade out of his jacket and tossed it playfully at her sweater, where it stuck like a burr. Leslie went from table to table, asking each party in her most apologetic voice to help her remove the grenade, but they were all German skinheads, and they ignored her. A few nights later she dreamed that S.R. was holding her hand, guiding her through the rubble of the Chechen parliament building in Grozny on a warm summer night. "See what those people have done?" he said, his sunglasses reflecting the stars. "Do you understand now why their trolleybuses mean nothing to us?" She awoke from each dream in a daze, feeling for several minutes that she had gained some key insight into his character. Then the sensation would fade, leaving her with a peculiar restlessness when she confronted his face, impenetrable and mocking, in the bureau drawer.

A few days later Leslie convened another meeting at her apartment. Lara and her daughters, the sad-faced man, and the old woman with the cane showed up within five minutes of each other, an hour late. There was no sign of the tall man or anyone else.

As Leslie ushered the small group to the kitchen table, Lara unveiled the name she had thought up for them: the Victims of the Second Moscow Trolleybus Bombing, or the ZhVMTV, as the acronym came out in Russian. She produced a bottle of wine and made a toast to mutual understanding among the victims of the world.

Leslie suggested they share their memories of the explosion. "It might be"—what was Russian for "empowering"?—"*upolnomochivayushchii*," she improvised.

"We picked ourselves up and rushed to the exit," Lara said, "but the door was stuck, so a man kicked it open. Was it you?" She frowned at Lev, the mustachioed man. He shook his head and looked down into his cup. "Well, some man did, anyway, and we helped each other out."

"We were choking, and our clothes were torn and smoky," said Vera, the old woman, in a whispery, excited voice. "None of us could hear a thing." She looked around the table, her eyes wide.

"Yes," Lara said. "That's what happened."

They all nodded gravely.

When Leslie urged them to explore their deeper emotions, Vera, her hands fluttering, protested that it depressed her to talk about the bombing. She suggested that they choose a topic to discuss at each week's meeting, such as cooking or tennis or tips on economizing in a democracy.

"I'm sure there are plenty of such clubs in Moscow," Lara said. "But this one is intended to help us cope with the tragedies of the past."

Leslie looked down at her lap, trying to hide her excitement. Lara got it!

"Well then, I'll be off," Vera said. "I've got to be up early to collect bottles." She downed the rest of her wine, stood up with the aid of her cane, and patted Leslie's hand. "Much luck to you!"

"As traumatic as the bombing was," Lara said after the old woman had hobbled out the door, "it was not nearly as painful an experience as the loss of my lifelong dream." Glowering at Lev, she began to tell him about the rigorous training required of airport ground controllers. Then she described her own inability to tell right from left. Finally, directing the full force of her stare upon him, she hurled these two elements of her story together like comets colliding in outer space. As Lara replenished their glasses, Leslie looked around the room at her kitchen friends and felt herself growing warm and content. Lev glanced at all of them sidelong, like a cowering puppy. Leslie found his shyness endearing, and she let her hand brush against his sleeve as she pushed the plate of cookies closer to the group.

In the final days of July, bombs exploded in railway stations in the southern Russian cities of Astrakhan and Volgograd, wounding several people. S.R. emerged from his mountain hideout to claim responsibility for the latest attacks, and he vowed to continue fighting Chechnya's battle for independence by sabotaging the Russian rails.

"The survivors of the trolleybus bombing on Prospect Mira," Leslie wrote, "do not understand why Mr. R. refers to his terrorist activities as a 'rail war.' My friends do not consider themselves warriors. These ordinary Russian citizens would simply like to ride a bus or a train without fear of being blown to bits."

The ZhVMTV's next meeting began with Lara retelling the story of her life's major disappointment and ended with Lev dozing off with his head on the table. Leslie was pleased by the companionship they had so quickly established, and the saga of Lara's thwarted career in aviation was compelling. But she worried that Lara's fixation on the past was preventing them from discussing other concerns. Surely there were issues Lev would like to share with the group; he might even like to confide in Leslie privately. Leslie herself was looking forward to the cathartic moment when she would reveal the shameful history of her real family to her surrogate one.

With the goal of helping Lara through her pain once and for all, Leslie convened the next ZhVMTV meeting in the shadow of the Worker and Collective-Farm Girl monument at VDNKh, the All-Russia Exhibition of Economic Achievements. It was a hot Saturday morning, the sun bleeding through a paste of smog, and Lara blotted her forehead with a handkerchief as Leslie led them down the long quadrangle, past grand, antebellum-style buildings with names like CHEMISTRY and ANIMAL HUSBANDRY etched into their stone facades. Women in their summer finery promenaded arm in arm, while men staggered beneath huge cardboard boxes stamped with primitive depictions of microwave ovens and washing machines.

"Here we are," Leslie said, stopping in front of a building labeled TRANSPORT.

"Oi." Lara's jaw quivered, as did her hearing aid's plastic cord. Her daughters latched onto her arms. Lev retreated a step. Leslie smiled gently, and he fell back into line.

"Lara." Leslie clasped the woman's shoulders and locked both of Lara's laser-beam eyes with her gaze. "It upsets me that you are still haunted by the loss of your lifelong dream. I sense it's keeping you from moving forward. I brought you here to help you gain a sense of . . . *zakritiya*."

Perhaps Russians didn't typically use "closure" in a psychological sense, but Leslie had made herself clear. "I will try anything," Lara said, sounding almost meek.

Once filled with exhibits touting the unparalleled ability of the USSR to shuttle its citizens to and fro, the Transport building was now divided into a warren of stalls, each crammed with imported household appliances and electronics. Shoppers shoved each other down the narrow aisles and pressed against glass display cases for the best views of American computers, German toaster ovens, and Japanese stereo receivers. Leslie found an open space for the ZhVMTV meeting at the back of the hall, near the garbage bins brimming with balled-up safety warnings printed in useless languages, and shashlik sticks sucked clean. Above the chaos, red and white tiles adhered stubbornly to Soviet glue, melding into a crude pointillism: ships steering firmly through the sea, trains snaking curvaceous mountains. Lara stared gloomily at the pockmarked jetliner overhead.

"Let's gather around," Leslie said, taking Lara's hand. The daughters linked up beside their mother. Lev closed the circle, one naked palm cupping Leslie's fingers, the other floating near the concave stretch of bronzed skin between Ksenia's low-hanging skirt and crop top. "Shut your eyes, please." Leslie peeked to make sure everyone complied. Lev's round face reddened, beading with oil like a bowl of borscht. "Now. I'd like us to imagine that we're passengers in an Aeroflot 747 that is descending into Moscow—all of us except Lara, who is below us on the ground, preparing to land the aircraft."

Lara let out a gasp and squeezed Leslie's hand.

"It's nighttime, and Lara is using lighted batons to guide the plane. The control tower is radioing directions into Lara's ears, and she is signaling right, then left, then straight ahead. She trusts her instincts—trusts her arms to go left, then right, then left again. The captain is at ease, knowing that his plane is in competent hands. He follows Lara's directions precisely: right, left, straight ahead." Lara's hand swung Leslie's in circles, looping the signals it had learned years ago. "The plane lands with a gentle bump and glides smoothly down the runway," Leslie said. "Lara breathes deeply and lowers her weary arms. She walks back to the airport, satisfied that she has executed her job perfectly."

Beside her, Lara was sobbing. Leslie and the two daughters enveloped her in a hug. After a moment, Lev joined the embrace. The shoppers elbowing by took no notice of the small huddled group.

Back at home, Leslie dashed off an account of the break-through. Inspired by Lara's bravery, Leslie told her readers, she planned to ask the group to help her confront her own demons. Next, shy Lev would have his turn.

When she turned in the column, Jason's mouth hung open for a long moment. "Maybe next week you could write about . . ." He appeared to be trying to grow a goatee, and the pale yellow tufts on his chin struck Leslie as somehow indecent. "About something else, you know, besides the trolleybus bombing and your, um . . . club?"

Riding home in a packed subway car redolent of sweat and pickled beets, Leslie fumed. Write about something else! Like what, the christening of a Dunkin' Donuts? Another noxious bus trek to Tchaikovsky's house museum? What could possibly hold more human interest than the survivors' attempts to navi-gate the tragedy? Nothing. Nothing, that is, except another bombing.

Leslie found herself gazing at an old man's dried-apple face floating in the middle distance. The man's eyes fluttered shut; Leslie's followed suit. Her stomach dipped as the train rose, the tan summer sky lowering to meet them. A garnet star glided by. The train had become a monorail, riding the lip of the Kremlin wall. A bearded man in black sunglasses and a jaunty beret muscled through the standing throng and sidled up to Leslie with a backward shove. "What is wrong with you Rus-sians?" S.R. whispered, his orange-scented exhalations tickling her eyelids. "Can't you see that all we want is to be left alone?" Leslie was paralyzed. "Next station: Black Cat Joint-Stock Company," a woman's voice intoned. S.R. pressed something into Leslie's hand and slipped away. Looking down, she found herself clutching a paper sack brimming with cookies.

Leslie's eyes snapped open. She gulped in air, shocked to find the train still screeching through the tunnel, her hands empty. The old man bobbed before her, working his lips, just another drunk held upright by the crowd.

"What's *he* doing here?" Lara cried as she filed into Leslie's kitchen with the rest of the ZhVMTV that night. She was scowling at the newspaper photo of S.R., which Leslie had attached with fast-food magnets to her steadily churning refrigerator. Before exposing her own vulnerabilities, Leslie had decided, she would assist the group in overcoming shared assumptions, ones perhaps as dangerous as those she had acquired from Grandpa Serge.

"That's a good question, Lara." Leslie poured a round of chilled kvass but left the Danish cake roll glistening uncut; she didn't want her audience floating on a sugar high during her revelation. There were already too many distractions in the room: Lev's sporty lime-green shirt, unzipped to reveal a thicket of auburn curls; Lara's naked right ear (her hearing aid had vanished); and the buttons pinned to Lara's and her daughters' chests, which read GET OUT NOW, ASK ME HOW. "I'd like us to think about that," Leslie said. "What *is* he doing here? Here in Moscow, that is."

"He's in *Moscow?*" Lara exchanged alarmed glances with her daughters and Lev.

"Oh, no. At least, I don't think so. What I mean is, why did he plant the bomb?"

"*He* didn't plant it," Ksenia corrected.

"His men, then," Leslie persisted. "What did he want, exactly?"

The group showed less evidence of strain than the sweating cake roll. Above their heads, the wall clock flicked away seconds like a timer on a game show or a bomb.

"To—blow—us—up—into—tiny—pieces," Lara said finally, her eyes zooming inward, marbles on a collision course with Leslie's nose. "That's what he wanted."

"Yes, yes—but why?"

"To attract attention to himself?" Irina offered.

"To attract attention to his *cause*," Leslie said, wishing she didn't sound like an exasperated schoolmarm. "Their fight for independence. Today, on the subway, it struck me: S.R. is a victim, just like us."

"A victim!" Lara barked.

"Lara," said Leslie. "We may disapprove of S.R.'s methods, but we can still appreciate his dedication to his cause. Just think of how the Chechen people have suffered in the war, yet still they continue their struggle. We, of all people, should understand." They looked at her glumly, bored history students. "Think of our own past," she hinted.

"Nineteen ninety-one!" Lara shouted, and slapped the table, beaming at her daughters like a matriarch on Russian *Family Feud*. Just the other day, while waiting for the nightly news, Leslie caught a snippet of the show. *What did we have shortages of ten years ago?* the pin-striped host had asked a family of five from Novosibirsk. *Cigarettes!* the teenage daughter shouted. *Sausages!* the son piped. But it was their mother, flushing with a survivor's proud certainty, who cried out the answer given by 68 of 100 randomly surveyed Russians: *EVERYTHING!*

"That's true," Leslie conceded. "But I was thinking of . . ." Blank stares all around. "Eighteen sixty-one? The emancipation of the serfs?"

"I wasn't alive then," Lara said, folding her arms over her chest.

"Oh, I know that." Leslie took her seat. She looked down at her hands. "There's something I've been meaning to tell you." Her ears scanned for some sign of interest—a tabletop vibration, an intake of breath—but picked up nothing. "My own ancestors owned an estate." She looked up. The other four were staring wearily at the opposite wall, like subway passengers; Lev was even swaying slightly. "They owned people, too. Other Russians. They kept them like animals."

The vacant expressions on the ZhVMTV's faces jelled and solidified until they were all perfectly still, like posed figurines. The clock quieted, receding against the gold-braid wallpaper as if painted there. Beads of perspiration thickened atop the cake roll like drops of glue; even Leslie's rattletrap fridge shuddered to a halt. The entire kitchen felt as lifeless as a diorama in a museum. The horror of her disclosure must have stunned them into fossilization. Nothing and no one in the room would ever budge again.

But even as Leslie despaired, she detected something stirring in the room—a twitch, a tremor, at the edge of Lara's mouth. The tic spread to the other side, becoming a matched set. Leslie watched as Lara's lips, straining against some unseen force, began to rise, stretching upward at a glacial pace. In a final burst of effort, the lips separated, carving craggy dimples in Lara's cheeks, revealing tiny rows of teeth in a palette of fall colors, like Indian corn. This, Leslie sensed with a chill of deep foreboding, must be Lara's smile.

"It certainly has been a hot summer." Lara's voice had turned singsong and unnaturally high, like the female announcer's on the metro when the tape spooled too quickly. On either side, the girls unleashed youthful versions of their mother's grin, accessorized with pearly teeth and lip-gloss shimmer. Lev rubbed his eyes with his fists and took a long swallow of kvass.

"Of course, Moscow is always hot in July, but this year!" Lara burbled. Above the Cheshire leer her eyes blinked like satellites, one pinned on Leslie, the other on Lev.

"That's absolutely true," Leslie said with fervor, hoping Lara was trying to change the subject out of tact. Did the ZhVMTV accept Leslie despite her family's ignominious past? "It's been terribly hot!"

"It makes you want to get away, the heat." The longer Lara's smile endured, the more painful it looked, as if engineered by unseen hooks and wires. "Don't you ever just want to get away? Say, to the great European capitals? Have you been to Paris? Rome? Istanbul?"

"Well . . . yes," Leslie confessed. "Of course, this time of year, it's just as ho—"

"What would you say, Lev," Lara interrupted as the eye that had been fastened on Leslie scurried to join its mate, "if I told you that in just a few months you could be running your own business, building financial security, and touring the world!"

Lev raised one eyebrow.

"Don't look so surprised! It's true!" Lara crowed. "With a little help from Travelife." She patted her button. " 'Get out now, ask me how!' That's the Travelife motto."

"I don't understand," Leslie said. What did any of this have to do with her ancestors? "What are you selling, exactly, Lara?"

"Social advancement, you might call it. Access to the finer things, freedom to go and come as you please—or simply to *go* and never return, if that's your fancy." She winked. Lev blushed.

From her lap Lara produced a purple brochure, the Travelife logo branded on its outer fold in yellow letters. Lev opened the brochure as if it were a delicate undergarment worn by a trembling lover. In the blurry center photo, the Eiffel Tower leaned like the Tower of Pisa.

"A woman I work with is halfway to Europe," Lara said, "and she's only been in business a few months!"

"You haven't given anyone any money, have you, Lara?" Leslie said, trying to channel her frustration into constructive skepticism and wrest back control of the meeting. She hadn't told them yet about Bloody Wednesday, the infamous Simonov-led revolt!

"The initial investment is quite reasonable," Lara told Lev.

"It seems like such a sudden change in careers for you, Lara," Leslie persisted.

Lara's smile cracked as it swung over to Leslie. "As you might recall, I've always been interested in air travel."

Now Leslie was the slow pupil. "I see."

"On Tuesday, when Alyona from the bread counter approached me, I thought, It's a dream come true!" Lara pulled the plate with the cake roll toward her. "Soon the girls will have their own businesses, too. It's so simple, anyone can do it!" She aimed the cake knife at the refrigerator. "Even him!" S.R.'s half-raised left hand signaled acceptance of the challenge.

Leslie jumped in. "Which brings me back to—"

"Maybe if he had his own business to occupy his time," Lara snarled, slipping back into her everyday voice as she sawed at the cake roll, "he wouldn't be so interested in blowing us up." The daughters doled out the plates; Lev took a bite with soundless gusto. "Give the bandits their freedom, I say."

"Really?" Leslie said.

"We've soiled our hands with their filthy lot long enough." Lara relaxed into a dreamy tone. "Murder's in their blood, after all."

"Lara! Surely you don't mean that."

"Of course I do." She brushed her hands together, raining tiny chocolate bullets onto the table. "In general, we Russians would be better off without all of these outsiders underfoot."

Leslie felt her neck stiffen. "I didn't know you felt that way, Lara."

"It's a well-known fact that people get along best with their own kind," said Lara. The daughters flashed wan smiles of assent. "Common traits bring you closer together. We Russians, for example. We like to improve our lives—but I know that's not for everyone. Take you, for example."

At the same instant she vowed to ignore the request, Leslie heard herself ask, "What about me?"

"There's a certain Americanness to your character, Leslie," Lara mused. "A nostalgic view of life, shall we say, an obsession with the past. We Russians don't have that luxury. We're people of the future."

"But Lara . . . I *am* Russian," Leslie reminded her. "Russian-American."

"Russian-American, eh?" Lara said. "Like a dictionary?"

The daughters giggled. Lev smirked.

"But I am," Leslie pleaded. How could Lara question this essential fact? It was the seed of Leslie's presence here, from which all else was supposed to bloom. "Remember, at the hospital? You said I was like family!"

"I was sick then, and weak," Lara said. "I'm better now."

"I know! Because I—"

"Because you helped me?" Lara lifted an eyebrow. "I'm much obliged, but my family can take care of me from now on. My Russian family."

"But Lara, I'm Russian, too!" Leslie cried. "As Russian as you are!"

"We have to go now." Lara pushed back the table. "We've got a Travelife conference in the morning."

Leslie leaped to her feet and snatched S.R.'s photo from the refrigerator. Tiny plastic hamburgers and hot dogs rattled to the floor. "I'm as Russian as he is!"

Lara stopped in her tracks; the others bumped up against each other. "You call him Russian?" she roared. "Look at that skin of his! Look at those shifty eyes!"

Leslie shivered. How could Lara see S.R.'s eyes behind the reflective lenses?

"I'll say one thing for him," Lara continued. "He knows who he is. He doesn't try to be what he's not." She brushed past Leslie. The girls and Lev followed her into the hallway.

"Wait!" Leslie shouted. "My grandparents—half of my blood—"

"Half of her blood," Irina echoed.

"A half-breed," Ksenia whispered. "Like a mutt."

"But I'm not a mutt!" Leslie protested. "I come from aristocrats!"

"What kind of fool do you think I am?" Lara shouted. The others were slipping out the door. "American aristocrats?"

"No, no! Russian aristocrats!"

"Russian aristocrats, eh?" Lara stooped to tie her tennis shoes.

"They were!" Leslie wailed. "We were! I am, I am!"

"Don't you know they were exterminated a long time ago?" Lara jabbed at S.R.'s photo, which Leslie still brandished in her outstretched hand. "Just like your friend will be," she growled, venom in her terrible eyes. She spun on her heels.

"You'll never get rid of me!" Leslie cried after Lara's retreating figure. "I'm more Russian than you'll ever be!" At this, she crumpled the photo in her fist, stifling sobs of rage.

In the week following the meeting, Leslie left several phone messages for Lara and her daughters; Leslie had bought them an answering machine at VDNKh, after Lara admired it, as a sort of congratulatory gift. Leslie ached to apologize for her elitist outburst, but they did not return her calls. She stopped by Produkti and was told Lara had quit.

Leslie slept fitfully and spent her days alternately napping and staring at her computer's blinking cursor. Each night she watched the news. Battle statistics from the south varied widely; the grainy stills of the dead and wounded reminded her of antiquated tintypes. She missed one deadline, then another, and still Jason did not call to inquire about her column.

On a warm mid-August day, the Kremlin's new security chief called for a cease-fire in Chechnya and for peace negotiations to settle the conflict permanently. Apparently, the television commentators scoffed, the mighty Russian army had been brought to its knees by a raggedy gang of bandits. The next day marked the one-month anniversary of the second trolleybus explosion. Just before the time the blast had occurred, Leslie pulled on some clothes and headed to the corner of Prospect Mira and Novoalekseevskaya Street.

At first she thought the small group hunched between the cars and pedestrians was a gathering of commuters waiting for the trolleybus. But as she crossed the street, Leslie realized she was approaching the other members of the ZhVMTV. All four bowed their heads as if in prayer. Ksenia clasped a bouquet of yellow roses. GET OUT NOW, ASK ME HOW buttons were fastened neatly to all four shirts and blouses.

"Hello," Leslie said, stopping at the edge of the circle.

"Oh," Lara said. The others watched her. "Hello there."

Lev and the daughters stepped aside, opening the circle like a gate. Leslie took a step forward and let her arm brush against Lev's. For more than a minute, the five of them stood squinting at each other's shoes. Then Ksenia tossed her bouquet onto the tracks.

"Maybe it would be better if the flowers were closer to the curb," Lev suggested. They all stared at him. He hadn't spoken since that first night, when he told them his name. "It would be a shame for them to be run over."

Ksenia retrieved the roses and dropped them at the curb.

"I'm surprised to see you all here," Leslie ventured.

"We wanted to make sure we had achieved . . . how did you put it?" Lara asked. " 'Closure.' " Her new, terrifying smile flickered across her face. "As we embark on our new lives."

"That's wonderful, Lara," Leslie said. She had helped this woman, whether Lara cared or not. That might have to be enough. But she had one hope left. "I want you to know I'm very grateful to the ZhVMTV, for your friendship and . . . Lev?"

She tried to catch his eye, but he was staring at Ksenia, who gazed stiffly over his shoulder as if she were about to be photographed. Leslie was dazzled by the girl's rare beauty: Ksenia was sphinxlike, with sun-burnished skin.

"Fate can surprise you sometimes." Lev shrugged. "That's all." A number 48 trolleybus was weaving toward them, and he followed it with his eyes, which then settled again on Ksenia. Gazing at Lev beneath fluttering eyelids, the girl rose up on her toes, extending her bare midriff like a telescope, entwining her slender arms above her head. She let out a low purr. "The cashier's office promised they would have our money today," Lev said.

"We'll go with you," Lara said.

Lev, Lara, Ksenia, and Irina waved at Leslie as they hurried toward the corner. Leslie watched them board, then stared after the trolleybus as it rattled down the street and melted into the haze of traffic. She looked at the flowers, wilting against the hot pavement. A film of grit already muted their garish yellow petals. Leslie felt she should do something to conclude the ceremony—cross herself, or dream up a secret wish. Finally she made a vague curtsy, looked quickly in both directions, and turned, hurrying toward home.

THE CONVERSION

On the night train from Moscow to St. Petersburg, Tom shared a second-class compartment with a young woman from Baku and an older American couple, missionaries from Grand Rapids, Michigan. The husband, a preacher, seized on Tom's modest knowledge of Russian and commandeered him as an interpreter in his attempts to convert the young woman. Tom was enchanted by the girl, who had a sinewy body, a musky smell, and a hard-shelled suitcase too big to fit beneath the lower bunks; it rested like a coffee table in the narrow space between them. Reclining on the upper berth across from Tom, the girl responded sleepily to his translations of the preacher's words.

"The old man said he knows many Russians are hungry for Jesus Christ," Tom said.

"Ask him for me, what does Jesus taste like?" the girl said. "Maybe if I knew, I would want to eat him, too."

"She wants to know how they satisfy this hunger."

"That's an excellent question," said the old man, who was lying on the lower bunk opposite Tom. His enormous belly was encased by an undershirt tucked into stiff dark jeans. His wife, reclining in the berth below Tom, resembled an oversized baby doll with her droopy gray-blond hair and frilly dress. Tom disliked them instantly. It might have been this preacher who converted the Russian man who in turn converted Heather, Tom's ex-girlfriend. As far as Tom knew, Heather was the first American to be converted to the Baptist faith by a Russian. Tom and Heather had lived together in St. Petersburg for almost two years, but he hadn't spoken to her since they broke up a year before. He'd heard from their mutual friends—the Russian couple he was on his way to visit—that Heather and the Russian had married and were now missionaries in Siberia.

"There are many ways to fill this need," the old man said. "Baptism, private contemplation of Scripture, and, maybe most important, consultation with a spiritual guide and with members of one's faith."

"He says Jesus tastes like a Snickers bar," Tom said. He had expected to struggle with Russian, not having spoken it since he left, but the words strung together without thought. He didn't trust them.

"Tell him Snickers are out of style," the girl said petulantly.

Soon she fell asleep. The preacher began to probe Tom about his own relationship with God. Why was he no longer a practicing Catholic? How had the Church failed him? Tom appeased him for a bit, then closed his eyes and feigned sleep. When the cabin had grown quiet, the only sounds the rhythmic clacking of wheels against track, he pushed close to the window and held back the stiff curtain. Above the forest, the sky shone a brilliant royal blue. It was early May, and in this northern latitude, daylight was intruding on the night. In places where the trees thinned, he glimpsed ramshackle wooden houses, somber and brown. A light burned in a window, and Tom imagined an old, bearded man resting his swollen feet in a basin, his wife filling it with water from a pitcher.

In the morning, Tom spotted his friends as the train pulled up to the platform. Dora and Anatoly sat on a wooden storage box in jackets and jeans, swinging their legs and scanning the windows. Dora was finishing an ice-cream cone. Tom wouldn't have known her if she'd been alone. She had cut her long dark brown hair to chin length, and jagged bangs fringed her forehead. Tom pounded on the window. They smiled and jumped to the ground.

"How wonderful it is to see you," he said to them in Russian, out on the platform, which was slick with recent rain. His long gray overcoat swung open, enveloping them. Over Anatoly's shoulder, Tom watched three big men in dark suits and satin scarves—red, purple, emerald green—hoist the Azerbaijani woman into the air. The missionaries tottered away, wheeling their suitcases around puddles. Tom released his friends to look at them, to let them look back. Dora towered over her husband; she had lost her tall girl's stoop. Her brown eyes, level with Tom's, darted across his face, as if he didn't match her memory of him. Her cheeks had hollowed; she was beautiful now, but less pretty than before. Anatoly was the same: eyes slit, mouth turned up into his usual sly grin, blond hair overgrown in clumps. They were glad he was here, yes, but it had been a long time since they'd seen each other or even talked, and he would have to work through their reserve. Of course, he should have expected that. Tom slung his duffel bag over his shoulder and latched his arms through theirs, blinking back tears. His friends, his friends. How wonderful it was to be with his friends again.

Sometimes Anatoly and Dora remembered to call the town where they lived Tsarskoye Selo—the former village of the tsars—but more often they fell back on its Soviet name, Pushkin; it was the poet's birthplace. Now they traveled there by suburban train, then caught a bus down the main boulevard. Dora and Anatoly lived in a subdivided brick house on a quiet street lined with fragrant lilac bushes, bowed by rain.

"So wonderful to be here again!" Tom said in Russian, masking his shock with heartiness as he strode through the apartment's two rooms, the floorboards squeaking under his bouncy tread. Everywhere he turned, he saw something from his and Heather's apartment in Petersburg. The computer. The pillows. The nonstick frying pan on the stove. Things they had brought from home or found in the city and used to make a life together. He and Heather vacated the apartment abruptly, separately; she had been the last to leave. She must have taken only her clothes and told their friends to help themselves to whatever they wanted.

"The computer works well?" His voice filled the small rooms. He talked too loudly when he got excited—Heather used to tease him about this.

"We stuffed two suitcases with things from your apartment." Dora leaned against the doorframe, relaxing into her familiar slouch as she studied him. Tom could so easily have fallen in love with her that it was a secret point of pride that he had not. She and Anatoly had been together since they were teenagers, and Tom was reverential about their bond. "And there was still so much we didn't take."

"Dora has the high score now on Tetris," Anatoly said, smirking.

"Ha!" Tom swept Dora into his arms and twirled her around. "That's my girl!"

She squealed as her stork legs, clad in narrow jeans, swung out behind her. "Let me down!"

"Tell me you missed me!" He glanced at Anatoly and was pleased to see his friend smiling with genuine affection.

"I missed you! I missed you!" Dora cried.

Despite his long journey, Tom felt restless, and he headed back outside with Anatoly to shop for supper. The steel-gray sky lowered as they hurried along the street; the wind whipped their jackets like flags. "It is a pity," Anatoly said, practicing his

English. "It was sunny for many days, but here you arrive with the clouds."

"I don't care. The only reason I'm here is to spend time with you and Dora," Tom said. "You don't know how often I think about you."

"As I think about you," Anatoly said, "though I have not written much."

"That's OK, man. That's OK." Tom had known his friendship with Anatoly and Dora would last even if they fell out of touch for long stretches of time. They were like family, but without the resentment or hurt feelings. They had met soon after Tom and Heather came to Russia; Anatoly was a reporter for the magazine where Tom worked as an editor.

Living in St. Petersburg had been Tom's dream, not Heather's, but it was she who talked him into leaving Seattle. She had been in law school, steady and reasonable in her desires, and her newfound restlessness excited them both. But that first summer in Russia, when Heather put off looking for a job and stayed inside cleaning and decorating, replacing the landlady's knickknacks with photos of family and friends, Tom worried she had overestimated herself, and her love for him. Afraid she might flee, he brought her whatever he thought would make her feel at home—Pyrex cookware, English-language novels, a plush terry-cloth towel.

She would need friends, too, so Tom invited Anatoly and his wife over for dinner and was relieved when they met with Heather's approval. That winter, to ease their commute, the Russian couple camped out in Tom and Heather's city apartment for nights at a time; they all stayed up late talking and drinking in the warm, cozy kitchen, with its slice of view of the frozen Neva. Heather found a job running the office of a British veterinarian who treated expatriate dogs and cats, and Tom relaxed. The four of them spent their summer vacation in Tsarskoye Selo. One night, locked out of the apartment after a drunken walk, he and Anatoly kicked open the padded door while the girls crouched in a corner of the hallway, shrieking with laughter.

Tom didn't expect they would have any trouble adjusting to being a threesome. In fact, he was certain his ten-day visit would be too brief. For months he had been thinking about moving back to Petersburg, settling down permanently. Running home after the breakup had been a mistake. He harbored a secret conviction that if he remained in America, he would always regard his time in Russia as the best of his life. He had forced himself to stop mentioning Russia to his friends and family, knowing how he sounded, obsessed, and how pathetic they must think him, as if it were Heather he pined for and not the freedom he had felt only there, unmoored from past and future. Without telling anyone, he plotted his return to Russia. If he felt the same after this trip, he'd come back to Atlanta and quit his job, sublet his apartment, buy a one-way ticket. His Russian would come back quickly, and he would rustle up some work; a decent-looking American guy, he could have his pick of women.

"It is good you're here." Anatoly's arm swung across Tom's chest as a bus trundled in front of them, rain hissing under its wheels. "Lately it has been gloomy for us."

"Gloomy? How so?"

"Dora and I have some problems . . ."

"I thought she seemed quiet."

"We'll talk later." The grocery store's red sign glowed through the mist. "After some wine."

Dora and Anatoly had been married for a long time, so of course they had troubles now and then. Anatoly worked too hard, and Dora felt neglected, and there was always the stress of not having much money. But even when they bickered or sat in moody silence, Tom had sensed a passion between them that he and Heather lacked.

In the kitchen, the three of them slipped into their familiar roles. Bending over the board that covered the footed bathtub, Tom sliced bread and cheese with one of his and Heather's steak knives. Anatoly chopped tomatoes, cucumbers, and dill for a salad. Humming, Dora tied on Heather's *Sweeney Todd* apron and seasoned the chicken, then started whittling the potatoes with a paring knife—Heather's old task; she had acquired the skill under Dora's guidance. Tom wanted to ask if they had heard from her, but he feared seeming eager for information.

Over supper at the small table, Tom told Anatoly and Dora about his media relations job at a software company in Atlanta. "My life is boring," he said, preparing to reveal his desire to move back to Petersburg. His heart thudded in anticipation of Dora's joyful cries and Anatoly's slow, sure smile. "Boring and unsurprising in every way." He waited, trying to diagnose their scraping silverware and downturned faces.

"What about all your girlfriends?" Dora asked finally, eyebrows raised. "Are they boring, too?"

Tom laughed. "Incredibly." He'd been on a few dates in Atlanta, with women from work who seemed interested only in their co-workers' foibles and the real estate they hoped to buy.

"You could bring home a Russian wife," Dora said. "We're interesting. Right, Tolya?" Their eyes locked.

Now. But again Tom hesitated, and Anatoly began to talk about the magazine. Circulation was low, ad sales down. Everyone expected layoffs.

"Maybe you should look around for a new job," Tom said. "I could help you with your résumé on the computer."

Anatoly was sitting in his familiar pose, legs crossed, one arm resting on his knee. He ate quickly and neatly, sliding food onto his fork with a slice of bread, and as usual he had finished first. "Perhaps I will leave Leningrad, go to Moscow for work," he said.

"Moscow?" Tom looked from Anatoly to Dora. "Really? You're thinking of moving to Moscow?"

Anatoly shrugged. "It depends."

"Depends on what?" Tom asked.

"It depends on Tolya," Dora said in her heavily accented English. She sat ramrod straight, gazing at her husband. "He wants the divorce."

Tom put down his fork and swallowed. "What?"

"Dora will tell." Anatoly fetched his Primas and matches from the top of the refrigerator.

"No," Dora said. "You want. You tell." She got up and left the room. Tom heard the bathroom door click shut.

"She is having an affair," Anatoly said. He lit a cigarette and squinted as he took a drag.

Tom shook his head. "Are you serious?"

Anatoly unlatched the window and exhaled through the crack. Dora had lit a few of Heather's vanilla-scented votive candles, and they trembled on the radiator cover. Outside, tree-tops bent and swooped against a turquoise sky. "She promises to stay; then she goes to him. This happens many times."

"But . . ."

"We went to get the papers for the divorce two weeks ago. The office was on holiday. Dora thought it was a sign, so we don't go back yet." Anatoly smiled. "Once again, I give her one last chance."

"Do you know the guy?"

"No. He lives in the city. I thought of talking to him, but . . . that would be crazy."

Dora returned, her face flushed and free of makeup. She looked younger, the age she still was in Tom's mind's eye. When she rested her hand on his shoulder, he squeezed it, not wanting to show her how hurt he felt, as if she had betrayed him as well. Tom's hazy dreams of moving back to Russia now struck him as a well-reasoned plan threatened, maybe already destroyed, by Dora.

"Tom, how long did it take for you to fall out of love with Heather?" Dora asked in Russian, not looking up from the dirty dishes she was stacking.

"I don't know." He wanted to answer the question to Anatoly's advantage, but he didn't want to come across as a lovesick fool. He had no idea what the truth was. "A few months, maybe?"

Dora nodded. "It's not so long."

"We weren't together so long. Three years. It's not—"

"It's not eight, hm?" Anatoly said.

After they had cleaned up, Anatoly uncovered the tub and Dora heated water in a kettle for Tom's bath. Alone in the kitchen, Tom undressed and climbed into the porcelain tub. He squirted aqua dish soap down his legs and arms, up his torso, and around his face, making a stick-figure outline. In a saucepan, he swirled hot water from the kettle with cold water from the faucet and drizzled it over his body. Beneath the trickling droplets, the apartment was still. A can of hair spray on the tub's ledge had a WALGREENS $1.49 sticker on it, and the lime-green towel he bought for Heather at an expensive boutique in Gostiniy Dvor rested on the lip of the sink. Each new discovery reminded him of what he used to have, what he wanted again: companionship, close friends who treasured his exuberance and loyalty.

Dora and Anatoly lay under blankets on the floor in the hallway, huddled away from each other; they had left the bed for Tom. His muscles unclenched against the cool sheet. An American-style pillow cradled his head. Another triumphant purchase for Heather; the pillows that came with their apartment had been twice the size and heavy as flour sacks.

Since leaving Russia, Tom had imagined Dora and Anatoly's lives continuing uneventfully, and nothing they wrote in their brief, rare E-mails suggested otherwise. When he proposed a visit, they had encouraged him. Why hadn't they warned him of their troubles? Of course, during his and Heather's second winter in Russia, when Heather became pregnant, they went to London to take care of it and didn't tell a soul, not even Anatoly and Dora. It was an insult, traveling to a Western country for an abortion. That was why they didn't say anything, Tom told himself.

Rain was rushing against the trees. Tom picked up a faint echo from the other side of the door: the rustling of clothes, limbs shifting against each other with deliberate slowness, striving not to be heard.

The sky was bright the next day as they walked through town, past prerevolutionary wooden houses caged by tall hedges, but a searing wind pulled tears from the corners of Tom's eyes. Waking at noon, he had called Anatoly and Dora away from their tea, determined that they would have a good day together.

Skirting Catherine the Great's gaudy turquoise-and-gold palace, they came upon the derelict Alexander Palace, where Nicholas II and his family lived in exile before being shipped to Siberia. A row of dirty columns, streaked with whitewash, curved along the broad front patio of the yellow stucco mansion. Scaffolding lined one wall, and a large sign painted in English read RESTAURATION OF THE BUILDINGS, but there were no workers in sight, and curtains masked the windows.

A turgid stream ran alongside the palace, widening for a small island. A white house the size of a single room, with a peaked roof and boarded door and windows, stood among spindly trees at the island's edge. Concrete pilings on each side of the water were the only remnants of a bridge.

"That's where the children played." Dora pointed at the house. "The tsarevich and his sisters."

"The little murdered children," Anatoly said, grinning at Tom, who took the cue and snickered.

"How can you joke about them?" Dora scowled not at Anatoly, but at Tom. He opened his mouth to protest, then stopped himself. Better she take out her anger on him than on her husband. "Such a close, happy family," she said, "killed in cold blood."

"So you're a monarchist now?" Anatoly said.

"It's only right that they should get a proper burial." She turned to Tom. "Next month, at Peter and Paul Cathedral."

Tom nodded; he knew about this. At the office, he checked the Web every morning for news from Russia. "Are you going to it?"

Again she glared at him. "How could I? I'm not some millionaire with ties to the president."

Tom looked away, sensing that Dora had detected the hopefulness swelling within him and felt compelled to puncture it.

Back in the apartment, Tom lay down for a nap, newly exhausted. When he rose, Dora and Anatoly were frying some kind of smelly tinned meat with rice. They had scrimped at the store, since he hadn't been along to pay, but he didn't mind; their cooking always turned out well.

After dinner, Dora lit candles in the main room while Anatoly prepared the tea. Tom sank back in the low armchair by the bed. The wire frame of the ceiling lamp was draped with a gauzy red fabric that puckered and gathered in his mind, becoming a skirt that swished around Heather's legs during a midnight walk down Nevsky Prospect during the White Nights.

"Heather's," Dora said, raising her eyebrows at the lamp. She had settled in front of the computer. Anatoly was stretched out on the mattress, flipping through a copy of *Newsweek* Tom had brought from home.

"I thought so. Are you still friends with her?" Again his

voice was too loud.

"I am." A red brick began its slow march down the computer screen, which bleached Dora's face an icy blue. "She visited a few months ago, while Anatoly was on an assignment."

"She came here? With her—with her husband?" The term sounded ridiculous in reference to Heather, even more so in the Russian instrumental case: *muzhom.*

"No, by herself. She was here for some sort of religious conference."

Tom thought of the hideous couple on the train. "How do you say convert?" he asked Anatoly in English.

"*Perekhodit'.*"

"Of course." He switched back to Russian. "Did she try to convert you?"

"Don't be silly," Dora said. "You know Heather better than that."

"I thought I did."

"You know, Tom, we never really spent much time alone, just Heather and me."

"I suppose that's true." Within their foursome, the language barrier had been greatest between the two women. And Heather used to feel intimidated by Dora, who was more self-assured, despite being the youngest of them all. "I'm sure you had a lot to talk about."

Dora's fingers tapped noisily at the keys. "What do you mean?"

"You know. So many changes in your lives."

"I suppose."

Anatoly was still looking at the magazine, but Tom sensed he was no longer reading.

"She probably had some good advice for you," Tom said.

The falling bricks froze on the screen, and Dora turned to face him. "Is there something you want to say to me, Tom?"

He scooted forward in the chair. "I don't know, Dora. Let

me gather my thoughts."

She shook her head. "You know, by the time Heather left, I understood better why the two of you broke up."

"Dora," Anatoly said. Rising from the bed, he picked up the teapot and glided out of the room.

"What's to understand?" Tom said. "She found God. She left me. End of story." He heard the click of the torch, then the burner igniting with a huff.

"Yes, but why?" Dora crooked her arm over the back of the chair.

"Some guy converted her."

"You make it sound like a magic trick."

He shook his head. "Anyone could've done it. No special skills needed."

"That's an ugly thing to say."

"It's the truth. She was looking for a reason to leave."

"And why do you think that was?"

"It wasn't very good for us, near the end."

"Not for a long time, according to her."

"Sounds like her Russian's gotten better."

"It's excellent. It's incredible, how she—"

"What else did she say?"

Dora surveyed him coolly. "She told me about your baby."

The candle flames beside Tom seemed to stop shuddering.

"She did?"

"Yes."

"She shouldn't have."

"Why not?"

"She should respect what we—what we—"

"I was shocked, Tom."

Anatoly appeared, sagging against the doorframe. "I thought we agreed," he murmured, but Dora's gaze remained fixed on Tom.

"We didn't want to— We thought it would be . . ." He

could think of no polite way to phrase what he and Heather had felt. Or, what he alone had felt?

"I know why you didn't tell us." Dora's eyes narrowed.

"OK, go ahead."

"You were trying to hide your shame."

Dishes clattered in the kitchen; Anatoly had disappeared again.

"Shame. Is that what Heather told you? Shame about what, did she say?"

"About Heather not wanting your baby."

Tom let his voice become stern. "Neither of us wanted it, Dora."

"But a baby would have made her stay."

"Dora, everything was fine until then!"

"Fine." She nodded. "That's what Heather said. The baby made her realize her life was too comfortable. And that you wanted it that way."

"I made her life comfortable?" He snorted. "That was a complaint? I suppose you agreed. That's how all men are, right?"

"I'm talking about you and Heather!"

"No!" Tom shouted. "You're mad because I hid something from you."

"I'm not mad about that." She stared at the rug. "That's between you and Heather."

"Not anymore, it isn't. Listen, how do you think *I* feel, hearing all of a sudden you might get divorced?"

"You think we should share everything with you because we're Russian?" Dora crumpled a cellophane cigarette wrapper in her fist. "Like workers on some communal farm?"

"God, Dora! This isn't about being Russian or American." He had forgotten her knack for teasing cultural stereotypes out of the most benign remarks. "It depresses me, it depresses me that there were secrets on both sides, that—"

"I know it's hard for you, Tom. You live in America now; you don't see us every day." Dora lowered her head, and her hair fell forward, shadowing her face. "You have no idea why this is happening."

"It's happening because you're—"

"Don't, Tom." Her voice sounded broken.

"You're doing what Heather did."

Her hair swung back and forth. Behind her, on the screen, the little colored bricks hovered in mid-fall. "That's not why. He's not why."

"Tell me." Tom smelled cigarette smoke coming from the kitchen, where Anatoly was evidently waiting out the argument. Tom sank to the floor and crawled over to Dora. "Maybe I can help."

"Tom, don't," she said, plaintive. "There's nothing you can do, I promise."

"Dora," he said. "Come on." He pushed back her hair. Her face was glazed with tears. He clutched her wrist and whispered, "Tell me."

"I really can't stand this, Tom!" she screamed, flinging his hand away. She pushed past him and grabbed a blanket and pillow from the bed.

He got up and followed her into the hallway. Anatoly was smoking at the kitchen table, in the dark. "What are you doing?" Tom said to Dora.

"I'm going to sleep." She folded the blanket in half on the floor and climbed inside. "I'm exhausted," she said, staring up at the ceiling with wide-open eyes.

Tom squatted beside her. "Sleep in the bed, Dora." Tom sensed Anatoly watching them. "Both of you. Take the bed. Let me sleep here."

"It's best for me to be here tonight. For everyone." She rolled away from him. Beneath the cap of dark hair, her neck looked pale and vulnerable.

"Maybe if we had told you—who knows, maybe things would be different," Tom said. "For everyone, somehow."

"It doesn't matter. I promise you it doesn't."

"Doesn't matter. God, Dora."

"You push too hard, Tom. People need room to breathe."

"Doesn't matter to who?"

"Tom, Heather's having a baby."

He laughed. "What?"

"She had just found out when she was here." Dora's voice was flat. "She was so happy."

He backed away. "We'll talk in the morning."

He could not sleep that night, with Anatoly across the room, Dora in the hall, himself the midpoint between them. He would *not* fault himself for making Heather comfortable in a foreign land; he would *not* fault himself for her restlessness, her convenient transformation, her betrayal. He refuted one point after another, but his thoughts kept coming back to London. Because they were visiting from another country, the clinic required Heather to stay overnight; Tom was turned out in the evening and wandered the neighborhood until dawn. On the plane ride back, Heather told him she had shared a room with several girls from Ireland and that one of their mothers sang them lullabies. It was soothing, she said. At the time, Tom thought she told him this to hurt him, to prove she had been fine without him. When she joined a Bible-study class soon after, he took it as further punishment. Now it felt like revenge again, that Heather told Dora after so much time had passed. Even Heather's new pregnancy felt spiteful. Of course, it had nothing to do with him, for which he was grateful; but he turned and turned on the mattress, finding no relief.

The next day when Tom rose, past eleven, Dora's bedding was piled neatly in the hallway.

In the kitchen, Anatoly looked up from a book. "She said she'd come back in one hour, but three have passed already," he said in English. "Probably she is gone until tomorrow or the day after."

"Fuck." Tom sank onto a stool. "I shouldn't have argued with her."

"She's angry with me, not you."

"Fuck, Tolya."

"She probably would have gone anyway."

"Maybe I should leave, go to Moscow for a few days so you guys can be alone when she gets back."

"Of course not," Anatoly said sharply. He looked past Tom toward the front door. The apartment lay in shadow. Beneath the rain pattering the roof, Tom could hear Anatoly's watch ticking. This is what it's like when I'm not here, he thought. "Of course we want you to stay," Anatoly said, gentler now.

Anatoly needed new shoes, so they ventured outside. The rain had stopped, but the trees dripped steadily, and as they walked, a musty odor rose up from Tom's dampening overcoat. At a bazaar tucked in the courtyard of the village's department store, Anatoly tried on a pair of running shoes, leaning on Tom to keep his stocking foot from getting wet. With their Velcro flaps and white piping, the blue sneakers looked cheap and girlish to Tom, and he felt contempt for his friend and for himself as he pushed a wad of bills into Anatoly's hands.

They bought fish at the market and stopped at the grocery store for wine. By the time they returned to the apartment, it was almost five o'clock; without Dora to protest the uncouthness of an early meal, they began to chop and fry. Over supper they discussed politics, American and Russian, then fell silent. They finished the second bottle of wine and went into the tangerine light for two more.

"I don't want a divorce," Tom said when they had resettled in the bedroom. *I don't want you to get a divorce,* he meant to say, but the wine made his Russian sloppy. In any case, it sounded truer this way, as if he were the one being left behind.

"We didn't want you and Heather to get divorced," Anatoly said.

"That wasn't the same. Not a divorce."

Anatoly shook his head. "Eight years. It's a foolish amount of time."

"You don't mean that."

Anatoly's face seemed to expand, then contract. He hid it in his hands.

"Tolya." Tom crouched on the floor beside him. "Tolya, it'll be all right." He braced his friend's shoulders. "Let's go find her, in Petersburg. Talk to the guy, or beat him up, or . . ." He could not imagine anything but comical and embarrassing scenarios.

"No." Anatoly's blue eyes fixed wildly on Tom. "Don't, please."

Tom laughed, startled. "Of course not. Not if you don't want to."

Anatoly stared at the floor. That was Tolya, Tom thought. Life washed over him, and he would never do anything to stop its flow. As he paced the room, Tom's eyes lit on the bookcase. There was Heather's *To the Lighthouse,* and the Russian copy of *Dead Souls* he'd bought in Seattle. *It's like a secret code,* Heather said soon after they met, flipping through one of his Russian books. *This mysterious part of you.* But the books were too difficult for him to read through; they always would be. He accepted this, as he accepted that twenty miles away, strangers slept in the bed where he coaxed Heather, on a night when they had no protection, by saying, *I'm beginning to feel like you don't want me anymore.* Weeks later he brought the pregnancy kit home and stood in the hallway, translating the American product's Russian instructions for her through the bathroom door.

Somewhere in Siberia, she slept beside her husband, their child curled against her.

He thought of his apartment in suburban Atlanta. The blinds shut tight, the ceiling fan slicing dead, hot air.

"Goddamn all this shit," he said in English, grabbing the pair of books from the shelf and slamming them on the desk.

Anatoly sighed and straightened, wiping his eyes on his sleeve. "What?"

"You guys have all this *shit*," Tom said. "All this shit that used to belong to me and Heather."

"Dora wanted it. I don't care for it."

"You don't?"

"It makes me crazy. She watches the computer all day instead of building her garden or speaking to me . . ." He shook his head.

Tom flopped into the armchair. He ran his hands through his hair and closed his eyes. He had reached a stage of drunkenness in which his best ideas would emerge unfiltered, if he could only hear them.

"Do you have a box?" he said finally. "A big one?"

Anatoly rummaged in the cabinet beneath the kitchen sink. He emptied glass and plastic bottles from a cardboard box, setting each one on the floor with excruciating care.

"OK." Tom kicked the carton into the middle of the hallway. "So we'll put everything in here."

"Everything?"

"Everything that used to be Heather's and mine. Then we'll throw it away."

Anatoly laughed.

"Seriously. We have to get rid of this stuff, Tolya. Don't you see?"

"Mmm . . ." He smiled, shook his head.

"It's tainted. By me and Heather. Your only hope is to get rid of it."

"Hope for what?" They were each speaking in their own language, like they used to do on deadline at the magazine. It worked because they both understood so much more than they could express.

"For a reconciliation."

Anatoly raised his eyebrows. "Between you and Heather?"

"Tolya. Between you and Dora."

Anatoly looked away. A muscle in his jaw twitched as steadily as a pulse.

"Listen: she has no *right* to give you a hard time about this." Tom pointed to the kitchen. "Now, you start in there, and I'll work in here."

After Anatoly shuffled off, Tom took the books from the desk and rifled through the drawers. He put everything he collected into the carton, setting the pillows beside it. Finally, he stood on tiptoe in the middle of the room—it throbbed around him in waves—and unhooked Heather's skirt from the lamp's wire frame.

Anatoly had added the frying pan and some knives to the box. Now he sat smoking at the kitchen table. Tom moved around the room, finishing the job.

With the pillows tucked under his chin, Tom lugged the box outside. Anatoly followed with the computer monitor. A cobweb snagged against Tom's face as he passed between two trees. The lilac bushes thrashed in the breeze, releasing their sweet, heavy scent into the yard, which glittered in the light of a three-quarter moon.

Anatoly veered off to the small garden beneath the kitchen window. He stood at the edge of the plot, staring at it over the top of the monitor.

"Hey." Tom came up to him. Except for some leafy weeds, the garden was barren, the earth cracked and pocked by the recent rain. "If we dump it at the curb, it'll be gone in a minute."

Anatoly didn't seem to hear him. He set the monitor on the

scrubby grass and rose slowly to his feet. Tom put the box down beside him and went back for the hard drive.

When he entered the room, he saw Anatoly through the window, a few feet away. He was digging in the garden, pushing a long-handled spade into the earth with the heel of his new shoe. He lifted a flat chunk of dirt and tossed it aside.

Laughing, Tom rapped on the window. Anatoly glanced at him and went back to his digging.

"Why don't we get rid of this stuff first," Tom said when he was outside with the hard drive. "Then we can turn over the garden, if you want."

"We get rid of it here." Anatoly's body was pumping like a piston. "In the hole."

Tom smiled. "You want to bury all this shit?"

He nodded.

"OK. We can do that." Tom squatted at the edge of the garden and watched his friend work.

Anatoly dug the way he ate, the way he walked and smoked: fast, with tidy, compact motions. He dug a couple of feet straight down and started to widen the hole, piling the dirt in even mounds along the perimeter of the garden.

When Anatoly paused to wipe his face with his sleeve, Tom rose and took the spade. He stabbed and lifted and tossed the soil aside, enjoying the prickling of sweat beneath his arms and the sticky coolness that rose on his face and back, as if the wine were oozing straight from his pores. Below the top layer, the dirt was rich and yielded easily, clotting and crumbling with his jabs. The rightness of Anatoly's plan surged through Tom. Dora would be furious, but she would have to admire the rashness of the act, proof of her husband's devotion and sorrow. In time, Dora would pass on the story of this night to Heather, who would laugh with tenderness and envy for the life she had abandoned.

When the pit had become a deep, rough square, Tom let

the spade fall to the ground.

Anatoly was stretched out on the scrubby lawn, hands folded on his stomach, a pillow tucked beneath his head. His ankles were crossed neatly, and the racing stripes on his new shoes glowed like comets. Panting, Tom slid off his overcoat and draped it over his friend. He took the other pillow and lay down beside Anatoly. A loamy smell rose up beneath the thick odor of lilac. As Tom's breathing slowed, he watched the trees' topmost boughs fanning black against the purpling sky. If not for the work they had yet to do, he would have drifted off to sleep. Which woman would he dream about under the shimmying canopy of trees? He could no longer conjure Heather's face. His mind's eye flickered over the sexy woman on the train, but it was Dora he chose. Eyes shut, she swayed above him to music only she could hear.

"This reminds me of the door," Anatoly said in English, his voice low and flat and perfectly sober. "Remember?"

"That night we were locked out of this place? When we kicked the door down?" Tom turned to show his friend his smile.

"No." Anatoly smiled back. "Not we." He nodded at Tom. "*You* kicked it down."

"Me? By myself, you mean?"

"Yeh. I told you wait, while I fetched the *slesar'*."

"The locksmith." Tom remembered now.

Anatoly looked up at the sky. "When I returned with him, the door was open. I saw you with Dora and Heather, drinking at the table. The door was broken. Smashed."

"Huh." Tom laughed. "I forgot about that."

"And the locksmith said, 'It is a pity they arrived before us, but at least they look like friendly burglars.'"

"I forgot about that, too," Tom said. "But I bought you a new door, right?"

"Yeh." Anatoly stood up and slipped into Tom's coat. "But

Dora and I, we preferred the old door."

Anatoly stooped to embrace the computer monitor and hoisted it, staggering backward. Grunting, he heaved it into the middle of the pit. It landed with a noise like creaking wood. He lifted the hard drive and hurled it. The metal made a gnashing sound. Tom stood and grabbed the frying pan, but Anatoly seized his wrist. Startled, Tom released his grip. Anatoly tossed in the pan, and it clanged against the computer.

Anatoly seized the pillows and lobbed them. He pulled Heather's apron and towel from the box and flung them in. Arms and legs cycling, he threw in the scissors, the stapler, the casserole dish, the three-hole punch, and the can of hair spray. He balled up Heather's skirt and tossed it. He dropped in two of Tom's old sweaters and a tie, blue with gold diamonds. The books sailed through the air, flopping awkwardly onto their spines. He bunched the knives in his fist and whipped them. He grabbed handfuls of spice jars, tapes, candles, and cosmetics and sprinkled them in the pit.

When he was done, he stood looking down, his body swaying with the phantom rhythm of his labor.

Tom joined Anatoly at the edge. Thick drops of rain thumped and pinged against the treasure arrayed on the dark, velvety soil. Tom wanted to call out to Heather and Dora, to summon them here to see the fruits of his love, sparkling in the crystalline air, splayed out for their pretty, bright death. But the women were as distant from him as the man at his side, and he could only sink to the ground in disbelief at how far they all had gone.

Anatoly took up the spade and hefted a mound of the displaced soil. As he worked, the hem of the long coat swayed behind him in the dirt, the sleeves shrouding his hands.

THE WOODEN VILLAGE
OF KIZHI

Tanya stood poised in the middle of the dark hallway in her blue nightgown, debating between three closed doors. One of them, she hoped, would lead to her mother—but which? Each door was caked with yellow paint and topped with a rectangular window. Light shone above the left and right doors, but the middle window was dark.

Tanya had awoken alone in her mother's narrow childhood bed, the vibrations of the train they rode north from St. Petersburg still humming in her bones. The night before, they had reached the end of their long journey from San Francisco to Petrozavodsk to find the entire household in bed, slumbering with the apartment's front door not only unlocked but ajar. *"Typichnii,"* her mother muttered as she carried Tanya over the threshold. Typical.

Now Tanya stood in the hallway, wondering where her mother had gone, wondering if it was night or day. They were arriving at the beginning of the White Nights, Galina told her on the plane. Instead of setting, the sun would dip to the horizon and bounce up again. Tanya couldn't be sure of anything here.

She heard a rustling behind the middle door and a sigh. Then—her mother's voice: "Mama, how can you expect me to change your pillowcases when you won't so much as lift your head?"

"Clean or dirty, when you're dying, it's all the same," a high voice crowed.

Tanya tiptoed to the door and twisted the knob. Her mother was easing into a straight-backed chair, red paisley pillowcases draped over her arm. Her warm brown eyes smiled at Tanya. "Here's our girl, Mama," she said.

At the far end of the room, heavy blankets thrown over the curtain rods blotted out the light. Pressing into the soft folds of her mother's nightgown, Tanya found herself at eye level with a brittle old woman who sank into a swelling mattress as if into a snowbank, her narrow face carved by shadow.

"After so many years, my Tanichka's finally come to visit me," the old woman said.

"Give your babushka a kiss," said Tanya's mother.

Tanya edged toward the bed and allowed her grandmother to peer at her with the dark, inquisitive eyes of a squirrel. Babushka did not seem particularly sick, though Tanya and Galina had come to Russia to help Aunt Masha and Cousin Liuba look after the old woman while she died. This was their first trip back to Petrozavodsk since moving to America six years before, when Tanya was just two. It was early summer, the start of school in San Francisco was months away, and Tanya's father had told them to stay as long as they were needed. Staring into her grandmother's glittering eyes, Tanya realized they might be gone a very long time indeed.

"She still looks like him," Babushka said.

"Mama!" Galina shouted.

Tanya backed away from the bed. Was Babushka talking about Daddy? Tanya didn't look like him; she couldn't.

"Well, it's true, isn't it?" Babushka said.

"Quiet, Mama," said Galina.

Papa: that was who Babushka meant. It had never occurred to Tanya that anyone besides she and her mother knew that her

Russian papa ever existed. They spoke of him only in private, and only in Russian, which Tanya's daddy didn't understand.

Galina nudged Tanya back toward her grandmother like a beach ball. Babushka grasped her chin with clawed fingertips. "Are you a good student?"

"Yes," Tanya said.

"Tanya reads beautifully," Galina said. "In English, of course. And you can hear for yourself how well she speaks Russian."

"Do you *read* Russian?" Babushka asked, pincers digging.

"We haven't gotten to that yet," said Galina.

"Maybe I'll teach you." The old woman's fingers snapped open. "We might just have time before I croak."

"Don't be vulgar, Mama," Galina said.

"They say I'm dying, Tanichka." Babushka winked at Tanya. "Rotting from the inside out, like a pumpkin."

Tanya recoiled. Her mother sent her off to get dressed. While Galina looked after Babushka, Tanya would spend the day at the lake with her cousin Liuba. Tanya rushed back to her mother's childhood room, where dust sifted through the sheer lace curtains like powdered sugar. Maybe they were going to Kizhi. But before changing, Tanya perched on the edge of a sagging beige armchair and fished a homemade cardboard coin out of the change purse in her teddy-bear backpack. Her grandmother's words rang in her ears: *She still looks like him.*

On an afternoon long before the trip was planned, while drawing at the kitchen table, Tanya had asked her mother to tell her about Papa. He died in Petrozavodsk when Tanya was only two years old, Galina said as her iron glided over one of Daddy's shirts. Tanya had heard this story many times. At night, with Daddy, Galina grew reserved; her English was poor, and she was easily flustered. But when she and Tanya were alone, she chattered nonstop in Russian, full of confidence and opinions. No, she didn't have any photos of Papa—Russians couldn't afford cameras, Galina explained. Yes, they had been very poor, but the three of them had been happy together. What was Papa like? Tanya wanted to know; she had no memories of him. Papa was kind and good, her mother told her. Was he smart? Galina cocked her head, frowning. "He was a very good speller," she said. "You never needed a dictionary when he was around."

Tanya coaxed her mother into drawing a picture of Papa. Bent over the paper, Galina sketched a miniature portrait. She drew strokes of long hair that bobbed up, curling at the chin. Two curlicues formed a narrow mustache. She gave Papa a thin face, a pointy nose and chin, and eyebrows that rose inward. He wore a skirt instead of pants, a blouse instead of a shirt; ruffles flared at his neck and wrists. A sword hung from his chest by a sash, and boots stretched above his knees.

Galina returned to her ironing, leaving Tanya to stare in awe at the drawing.

"Where did he die?" she asked.

"Papa died at work, at the ice-cream factory in Petrozavodsk," her mother said.

"How?"

"He fell into a vat of ice cream and drowned."

Tanya's legs kicked in a frenzy beneath the kitchen table; this was her favorite part of the story, and in her excitement she grew bold. She asked her mother to draw another picture. A picture of Papa in the ice cream.

Galina stared at her. Without a word, she returned to the table. Beneath the first picture she drew a bucket—no, a vat. A ladder led up its side. She sketched wavelets of churning ice cream and, poking out of them, a pair of upside-down pants topped with triangle-shaped shoes. "Those are Papa's legs," she said, pointing with her pen tip. Then she returned the story to its familiar track, telling Tanya about the handsome American tourist she met after Papa's death and married in an ancient

wooden church on one of the islands of Kizhi. That was
Tanya's daddy.

Soon after, at school, they read the stories of Aladdin,
Beauty and the Beast, and Cinderella, and Tanya's teacher as-
signed the class to make their own magic objects, like the lamp,
the ring, the slipper. Tanya traced around a quarter and cut out
a cardboard coin. She glued the drawing of Papa in his skirt to
one side and the drawing of him drowning to the other. "Is
that man swimming, Tanya?" her teacher asked. "Who is he?"
Tanya watched her classmates pass the coin from hand to hand.
"An angel," was all Tanya would say. If Daddy found out about
the pictures of Papa at parent-teacher conferences, he might be
upset.

Now she held up the side with Papa in his skirt to the wall
mirror. Her hair was straw-colored and straight, not dark and
curled, and her nose was round, not pointed like Papa's. What
resemblance did Babushka see that Tanya could not?

Petrozavodsk was muddier than San Francisco, the pastel homes
set back from the street, shabby and shy. Oval clouds strung the
gray-blue sky like beads. Tanya skipped to keep up with her
cousin Liuba, who tottered swiftly along the sidewalk in high
heels. Liuba was older than Tanya expected, an unsmiling
teenager with a long ponytail sprouting from the side of her
head.

Tanya could hardly believe she had lived in this place for
two years; it felt completely foreign. Store signs were printed in
the Cyrillic letters she'd seen in her mother's newspapers at
home. Pictures—tomato, hammer, shoe—gave clues to the
signs' meaning and added cheer, like drawings in a picture
book. They passed few men, but many women, pushing old-
fashioned baby carriages, gathered at bus stops, toting net bags
sagging with potatoes and onions. The women spoke to each

other with bowed heads, their words swathed in gauzy white, as if each exchange cradled a delicate secret. Tanya had expected Russian men to look like Papa, with bobbed hair, swords swinging alongside their skirts, but they looked like American men in their jeans and short haircuts. Her mother had told her that in 1991, the year Tanya was born, everything in Russia changed. When she drew the picture, she must have been remembering the way things used to be.

"Two Eskimos," Liuba said. Tanya, thinking she was describing the two of them side by side in the crisp air, giggled with relief that her cousin had finally spoken to her. But Liuba was talking to an old man who gazed at them through the scratched plastic window of a square white hut. "This is my cousin." Liuba pointed at Tanya. "She's visiting from California."

"Oh, an American." The man passed two foil-wrapped ice-cream bars through a hole in the window.

"No, she's Russian." Liuba shook her open palm at Tanya until she thought to hand over some of the worn but colorful bills her mother had given her before they left the apartment. "She only lives in America."

"I'm an American." Tanya was indignant. "My daddy's American." Their frowns told her how strange the word daddy sounded, sandwiched between Russian words.

"But your papa was Russian," Liuba said.

"Russian, American, what's the difference?" the man said with a kind smile. "We're all friends now."

When Liuba turned on her heels, Tanya ran after her, though she would have liked to linger. She wanted to ask the man if he had worked with Papa at the ice-cream factory. How strange it was to think she and her mother had lived with Papa in this very town.

They descended a hill flanked by tall apartment buildings, and the lake stretched out before them, wide and gray. Along the boardwalk, they passed some fishermen, legs dangling over the retaining wall, lines disappearing into the water. Farther on, two steel stick figures cast a metal net into the sky.

The boardwalk curved, and Tanya saw a black tree standing stark and leafless in the grassy field. As they drew close, she saw that it was not a real tree, but a statue of one, made of something heavy, like the clay she used in art class, and painted black. Anchored in some rocks, the tree statue rose as tall as the leafy trees in the grove beyond the field; its limbs curved and tapered like tentacles and tusks. Bells swung from the highest limbs, tinkling in the breeze from the lake.

Something white and glossy protruded from the tree: a replica of a human ear, about the size of Tanya's head. Liuba went right up to the ear and whispered something into it. Above the ear was a placard with a Cyrillic inscription. Tanya wanted to ask Liuba what it said, but she was ashamed of revealing that she couldn't read Russian.

"We've got a lot of statues in Petrozavodsk," Liuba said. She plopped down on a bench facing the tree and finally—Tanya had been waiting so she could start hers—ripped the foil from her Eskimo. "New ones and old ones. They used to make all the statues here, and the cannons, too. This isn't like America, where everything's new and artificial. Do you know what artificial means?"

"Yes," Tanya said. She sat down beside Liuba. Beneath the Eskimo's brittle chocolate crust, the cold vanilla was lush and creamy. Tanya wondered what it would feel like to be trapped in a vat of ice cream. Had Papa really drowned, or had he frozen to death? She practiced a question in her head before asking it aloud: "Did you know my papa?"

"Yes," Liuba said without pause. "But I'm not allowed to talk to you about him."

Tanya mulled this over. "Why not?"

"My mama told me not to. On account of what happened

to him."

"On account of how he died?"

Liuba shot her a vicious glance. "Are you trying to trick me?"

Tanya shook her head.

"My papa was a war hero." Liuba pulled a golden locket from beneath her shirt and dangled it in the air. "I've got a photo of him in here."

Tanya munched her ice cream in silence. Russians couldn't afford cameras, her mother had told her. Liuba was probably lying. Russia was a land of stubborn, hopeless people, Galina liked to say, their own relatives most of all. She and Tanya had been lucky to escape. "Where's Kizhi?" Tanya asked.

Liuba made a sweeping motion with her ice-cream stick, the gesture encompassing the entire lake.

Tanya squinted at a dark strip of land between water and sky. "Are we going there?"

"Not today."

The night before she and her mother left San Francisco, when her father tucked her into bed, Tanya asked him to tell her about Kizhi. Her mother's offhand mention of a church and some old buildings hadn't satisfied her, and she could always count on Daddy to tell her in careful detail whatever she wanted to know. Kizhi was a village-museum, her father said. A number of ancient, intricately carved wooden buildings— peasant homes, churches, a bathhouse—had been gathered from all across the region of Karelia and spread along the length of an island.

"You'll travel there by boat," Daddy said, "and the first thing you'll see is a magnificent church with dozens of onion domes made out of tiny wooden tiles. The domes will shine so bright you'll think they're made of silver." Her father's voice was even and soothing, like the narrator of a nature film. His arms cast hulking shadows against the wall. "There are no nails holding it together."

"Why doesn't it fall down?" Tanya asked.

"The pieces interlock, like a puzzle. The church is held in place by its own weight."

"And that's where you and Mama got married? In the church?"

Her father stared at her. His eyes were pea-sized behind his thick glasses, and Tanya felt like a grotesque insect magnified by his lenses to human size. "Sure, that's it," he said. "We got married at Kizhi, and I took you home with me." He kissed her on the forehead and rose to leave. "And the three of us lived happily ever after."

Now Tanya imagined she was surveying the horizon through her father's binoculars, zooming in on the island, the silvery domes. Her parents ran from the church onto a field of tall green grass that bowed in the wind, Daddy in a tuxedo, Mama in a white dress and a long veil that flew behind.

The last of her ice cream was melting. Tanya licked the stick clean and stuffed it into her pocket. Her fingertips brushed the rough, curved edge of the cardboard coin. Kizhi was the place Tanya's real life began, her life in America with Mama and Daddy and all of her friends. But as she rubbed the coin with sticky fingers, it was Papa she thought of now.

"Repeat after me," Babushka said.

Sitting at her grandmother's bedside, Tanya echoed the familiar sounds—*zh, kh, sh, ts*—and tried to match them with the strange symbols Babushka had written in a long column on a sheet of paper. She was frightened of the old woman, who seemed so chatty and sharp despite the doctor's predictions of imminent death. Tanya clutched the Papa coin in her pocket, hoping it would help her.

The telephone rang in the distance, a primitive jangling,

and Liuba popped her head into the room: "It's Tanya's papa."

Tanya froze. Liuba was playing a prank. She knew very well that Papa was dead.

"It's expensive to call all the way from California, dear—run along," said Babushka.

Daddy! Tanya ran to the dark hallway and pressed the heavy receiver to her ear. "Hi, Daddy," she said, breathless.

"Hi, sweetheart," her father said. "How are you?"

"Fine." Tanya winced. She had almost said *khorosho*. What if they stayed in Russia so long that she forgot how to speak English?

"I miss you and your mom already. How's your grandma?"

"OK."

"Is your mom there?"

"She already went to bed."

"Don't wake her, then. Just give her my love."

"OK." Tanya was relieved. Sometimes her parents enlisted her as their interpreter. Though they never fought—Tanya viewed their careful politeness as the purest form of love, like that of Snow White and her prince—she worried that one day she would make a translation mistake that would lead to a fight, even divorce.

Her father wanted to know if she'd gone to Kizhi yet.

"No." She was afraid to say more, for fear she would start to cry.

"Well, make sure you go see it for me. You can't leave Russia without going to Kizhi."

Tanya nodded.

Back in bed, burrowing against her mother's warm body, Tanya felt sorry for Daddy, all alone at home. Once, she had asked him where he met her mother—meaning, where in Petrozavodsk. To her surprise, he sat her on his lap in front of his computer and circled the mouse over its pad. Words and colors flashed across the screen; then photographs of women appeared. Rows and rows of women with red lips and fancy hairdos scrolled by in little boxes, labeled with names: MARINA, ELENA, NATASHA, IRINA.

"This is where I found your mother." The boxes on the screen stretched like stars across his lenses. "I got her address here and wrote to her, and then I visited her. But don't tell Mom that I showed you. She takes a more romantic view."

Tanya thought of all the pretty Russian ladies on Daddy's computer. If Babushka took a long time to die, they might be here for a year, even longer. Tanya would have to go to a Russian school with Russian children and Russian teachers, and for the first time she would be a slow reader, a dunce. When Tanya and her mother finally went home, they would find another Russian woman married to Tanya's daddy, another little Russian girl sleeping in Tanya's canopy bed. By that time, Galina's English would be long gone, Tanya's too, and there would be nothing they could say to win her daddy back.

The next morning as they lay in bed preparing to get up, Tanya told her mother about Daddy's phone call. "He said he misses us," she said.

"Of course he does," Galina said. "And we miss him, don't we?"

"He said he wants us to come home right now," Tanya improvised. "He said we have to come home today because he's not feeling well."

Galina looked at her. "Tatiana O'Shanahan. Daddy said nothing of the kind, did he?"

Tanya grinned and shook her head.

"Lying is an unattractive habit in a young lady." Galina smiled grudgingly. "Especially when you get caught." They giggled together, nestling close. "Which reminds me."

"What?" Tanya said.

"Your cousin Liuba." Galina drew back to let Tanya see her whole face. "She's a liar and a know-it-all. You shouldn't take anything she says seriously."

Tanya was spooked. "Can I stay home with you today?"

Galina shook her head. "You wouldn't have any fun cooped up here at home, and I don't need a little girl underfoot. Taking care of Babushka is hard work."

Tanya made a pouty face, but her mother was unmoved. "None of that lip," she said, throwing back the covers. "Up we go, ready or not."

Tanya hated the long days she and Liuba spent at the lakeshore, loitering behind the low concrete building where tickets to Kizhi were sold. Liuba stood by the building with her tall, sullen boyfriend, Volodya, and his brown horse, while Tanya, who was afraid of the horse, sat across the driveway on a stone bench, reading a library book from home. Sometimes American children ran up to Volodya's horse, their English whizzing through the air like tiny poison darts: "Mommy, Mommy, can I? Can I, Mom, can I?" For five rubles, Volodya led the kids in a slow circle around the driveway while their fathers filmed them with video cameras. Down on the dock, tourists filed on and off the big white boat.

You can't leave Russia without going to Kizhi, Daddy had said. Tanya knew better than to take the warning literally, but she accepted it as a superstition—like her mother's insistence that they sit down in the hallway for a moment before leaving on a trip. One day, Tanya knew, Liuba would disappear into the concrete building, not to use the washroom, but to buy tickets for their voyage across the lake. Then Tanya could go home to Daddy, and Papa would be nothing more than her guardian angel again. Here in Russia, she kept thinking of him as a real person, and she was tired of the stupid questions that came to her as she read: Did Papa wear a skirt at home, slacks at the factory? Did he used to bring home ice cream? And why wasn't

Liuba allowed to talk to Tanya about him?

It didn't help that Babushka wasn't getting any worse. Though bedridden and uninterested in food, the old woman remained perfectly capable of bossing Galina during the daytime and quizzing Tanya on the alphabet each night. Galina's long days at Babushka's bedside left her as irritable and fussy as a child, and at dinnertime she bickered with Liuba and Aunt Masha. "She'd better hurry up already," she said on the sixth night of their visit.

"The doctor said—" Liuba said.

"The doctor said Mama'd be gone a month ago," Galina snapped.

"If you can't afford to stay on, Galya, by all means . . ." said Aunt Masha. She was a heavy, slow-moving woman who didn't speak to Tanya directly, as if she didn't trust her niece's knowledge of Russian.

"I've told you money's not an issue," Galina said. "We'll stay as long as we're needed."

"What if she doesn't die, Mama?" Tanya asked.

They all looked at her.

"Tanya needs some more beets." Aunt Masha lumped a spoonful of the steaming mash, leftovers from the hospital cafeteria where she worked, beside the one Tanya had been flattening with her fork.

As much as she wanted to go home to Daddy, Tanya was secretly beginning to enjoy her nightly reading sessions in the sickroom. At first she had tried to fend off Cyrillic, but it was no use: she was simply too smart. She could identify all of the letters now and piece together short words like *khleb* and *obuv'*—bread and footwear—when she saw them on the street. Her grandmother goaded her on, patting her hand and telling her how much smarter she was than Cousin Liuba. "Must've got it from him," Babushka said, looking at her granddaughter sidelong, and Tanya felt a little spark of satisfaction.

Each day at noon, Liuba and Volodya ate lunch in a bar next to the ticket office and afterward brought food to Tanya and the horse: bread rounds crusted with orange caviar or sweaty ham, lukewarm mango nectar in a waxy cup. The bar was not a place for children, Liuba never tired of explaining.

You're not so smart, Tanya thought. Babushka told me.

Feeling peevish while waiting for her rations, she wandered across the driveway into a circular park shielded from the street by teardrop-shaped trees. In the center of the park, a statue of a man on a pedestal towered above Tanya. The man wore a dress and knee-high boots. A sword hung from a sash at his waist. His hair curled up from his neck, and he had a thin mustache. His finger pointed straight at Tanya.

She took out her homemade coin and held it up against the white sky, letting it hover like a pale daytime moon. She looked from the picture to the statue, then back again.

Papa and the statue could have been twins.

Tanya copied the pedestal's engraving into her notebook, her newfound knowledge shimmering before her: Papa was a city hero, his tragic death at the ice-cream factory commemorated for eternity with a magnificent statue. Why had her mother never told her that he was famous?

When Tanya and Liuba returned home, cackling laughter pealed from Babushka's bedroom. "Still tough as a horse," said the doctor, a woman as old as Babushka, when she emerged to accept tea and a cigarette in the kitchen. "Will be until she breathes her last."

"Which will be . . . ?" Galina asked.

The doctor exhaled a cloud of smoke. "Any day now."

Galina eyed Tanya. Any day now they could return to San Francisco, her glance said. Liuba watched them, her head resting on the table.

"Having a nice visit, Galya?" the doctor asked. "Catching up with old friends?"

"Mama takes up most of my time." Galina hugged Tanya. "It's hard for us to be away from Cliff." Hearing Daddy's name made Tanya feel superior to Liuba, whose father had died a long time ago in a war whose name Tanya could not remember.

"Cliff, that's right." The doctor pronounced Daddy's name "Cleef." "Quite a whirlwind romance, that was." Smirking, she reached for another cigarette.

"Tanya and I thank God every day that we got out of here," Galina said with a sweet smile. She emptied the ashtray into the bucket, then let it clatter into the sink.

Tanya decided not to ask her mother about the statue. Instead, after supper, she presented her grandmother with the transcription:

ИМПЕРАТОРУ ПЕТРУ ВЕЛИКОМУ

"Marvelous," Babushka said. "You're doing homework. Sound it out, like I've taught you."

"Ee-em-pe-ye- . . ."

"That's right, keep going."

Slowly, Tanya pieced the words together: *"Imperatoru Petru Velikomu."* To Emperor Peter the Great. Peter the Great?

"That's right," Babushka said. "Peter the Great."

Was Papa's name Peter? Tanya had never thought to ask. "Who was he?"

"You mean to say— Shame on your mama for not teaching you the history of your homeland! Why, he's only the best tsar ever, and the founder of our town—Petrozavodsk, don't you see?" Babushka tapped the page with her pencil. "Peter's factory."

"The ice-cream factory?" Tanya said, clinging to her beautiful idea.

Babushka stared at her. "You mean where your papa

worked?"

Tanya nodded.

"No, darling. Not the ice-cream factory. They made guns at this one."

Tanya thought this over. "Babushka, what did my papa look like?" she asked, searching the old woman's black-marble eyes.

"You mean you've never seen any pictures of him?"

"There are pictures?"

Babushka snorted; her hand fluttered in the air. "Bring me that box from the shelf."

Tanya retrieved the dusty black shoebox and placed it on her grandmother's lap. Babushka lifted the lid, releasing a sour smell. Setting aside a stack of letters written on brittle paper, she held up a photograph. "This is your mother, in high school." Galina pouted, tragic and gorgeous, in the formal black-and-white portrait. "Always a beauty, eh?" Babushka turned to a photo of men in uniform. "Your uncle Fyodor is in this one, somewhere." That was Liuba's father, Aunt Masha's dead husband. "Relatives," Babushka said, flipping past grainy photos of scowling peasants.

"Aha." The old woman held out a picture to Tanya.

A man rose from a pool edged by rocks, his tan, muscled torso twisting up from the water. He wore nothing but green underwear, which flickered in a wavy band just beneath the pool's surface. His legs were rippling shadows. The man's slick, wet hair looked like porcupine quills. His clean-shaven face tilted up, toward the person with the camera, and his eyes said something both hard and tender to that person while his rosy lips remained firmly shut.

"That's your papa, swimming at the lake." Babushka's voice was low. "See how good-looking? Such muscles. He was in that lake so early in the springtime, I used to tell him his blood would freeze." Babushka handed Tanya the photograph. "Now do you see what I mean?" She outlined Tanya's lower lip with a fingernail. "There he is." Her squirrel eyes gazed deep into Tanya's. "And there, too." Tanya didn't dare breathe.

The old woman shook her head. "Now run along, and don't tell your mama I gave you that picture. I want to spend my final days in peace."

The next morning at the lakefront, Tanya stared steadily at the photo, tucked within her library book, and took her home-made coin out of her pants pocket. Papa was not a mustachioed gentleman with curled hair and a ruffled collar. He was an ordinary man like Daddy, but handsome, with his suntan and muscles, and eyes that looked right inside her. Next to the photo, Mama's drawings were cartoons. Not wanting the coin to touch her anymore, Tanya tucked it into her change purse.

Tanya framed her own face in the mirror of her mother's compact, which she'd hidden in her backpack that morning. In San Francisco, grown-ups were always telling Tanya to smile. Now she flushed, for her mouth *was* just like Papa's, lips tight at the edges, spilling over in the middle. They both had serious eyes, too, set deep within their faces.

"We're going for a walk," she heard Liuba say. Tanya snapped the compact shut and closed the book on the photo. Liuba was perched above her on the horse; Volodya held the reins. "You have to come with us."

"Where are we going?" Tanya asked as Volodya led the horse across the grassy field. No one answered. Maybe it was a surprise. Maybe they were going to Kizhi.

The white touring boat was gliding toward the dock, but the teenagers passed it without a glance. Volodya steered the horse toward a grove of trees and helped Liuba to the ground, then tied the reins to a tree. "We're going to go have a private conversation," Liuba said to Tanya. "You wait here. Don't move!"

Tanya and the horse watched each other as the teenagers disappeared into the forest. Then Tanya headed toward the boardwalk. In the center of the field was the black statue of the tree she'd seen on her first day at the lakefront with Liuba. Two boys stood smoking nearby; they paused in their conversation to watch Tanya. She looked at the tree's big white ear, then at the plaque above it. She made out the first word and slowed down to read the next two: PROSHEPCHI ODNO ZHELANIYE.

Whisper one wish.

The boat had reached port; tourists were waiting at the boarding plank. She glanced behind her. The horse stood alone, still as a statue.

Inside the building, Tanya slid her remaining fistful of Russian bills through the hole in the plastic window. A book obscured the cashier's face; on the cover, a large tanned man in a torn shirt kissed a pale woman in a scarlet dress. Tanya shouted, "One ticket to Kizhi, please!"

The woman lowered her book with unbearable slowness and gazed at Tanya through an enormous pair of orange-tinted glasses. "Where's your mama, little girl?" she asked.

"At home."

"What about your papa?"

"He's dead." Tanya lifted her chin.

"Oh, dear. Then who's taking you to Kizhi?"

Tanya tried to stare the woman down.

"Little girl, you can't go on the boat by yourself." The woman pushed the money back through the hole. "Tell your mama that an adult needs to take you."

"But my daddy told me I had to go."

The woman wrinkled her nose. "Your . . . *deh-dee?*"

Tanya sighed. "My *daddy*. In *America*."

"Little girl, even foreign children must be accompanied by a parent." The woman tapped a sign posted on the window. It was covered with black Cyrillic letters smaller than ants. "Run along, now." She picked up her book.

Tanya jammed the money in her backpack and dashed outside. The crowd was filing onto the boat. She would slip among them, unnoticed.

Volodya was galloping across the field on the horse, and Liuba ran behind him, her red jacket ballooning like a cape, her locket bouncing against her chest. "You're in big trouble," Volodya called down, addressing Tanya for the first time ever, then trotted away.

"Didn't I tell you not to move?" Liuba yelled. Her ponytail had come loose. Her nostrils flared as wide as the horse's.

"I want to go to Kizhi," Tanya shouted.

"No way, not after you ran off like that!"

"You *have* to take me. A grown-up has to take me."

"Don't you know anything? *I'm* not a grown-up. Why do you want to go there so badly, anyway?"

"I want to see the church."

"Why do you care so much about a stupid church?"

"That's where Daddy and Mama got married."

"Is that what your mama told you?" A smile crept to Liuba's face. "That they got married at Kizhi?"

Tanya could only gape at her cousin.

"What did your mama tell you about your papa?" Liuba asked. "What did she say about how he died?"

"He died at the ice-cream factory."

"An accident at work?" Liuba giggled, covering her mouth.

"He fell into the ice cream—"

Liuba's eyes bulged open, and she shrieked.

"He fell into the ice cream and drowned!" shouted Tanya.

Liuba laughed so hard she doubled over; she laughed so hard she made no sound, and her wide-open mouth was ugly and huge. Enraged, Tanya waited with clenched fists for her to stop.

"So, do you want to know the truth?" Liuba said when her

last gasps had subsided, wiping tears from her eyes. "Do you want to know how he *really* died?"

"Yes," Tanya shouted, then pursed her lips, ashamed of admitting that she doubted her mother's story, that she wanted to know the truth about Papa more than she wanted to go to Kizhi. More, even, than she wanted her daddy.

"Well, too bad." Liuba grinned. "Because I'm not allowed to talk to you about him."

"If you don't tell me," Tanya blurted out, "I'll tell Mama that you left me by myself, and that you went into the trees with Volodya for a long time, and that I started crying"—she paused to catch her breath, relishing the moment: Liuba had gone white—"and that I went to look for you, and"—she thought of Papa, poor Papa flailing in the ice cream—"and, and that I almost fell into the lake and drowned, and if I did, it would have been all your fault."

"I'll start at the beginning," Liuba said.

Tanya's usual lunch was spread out before her, but for the first time she was eating it inside the bar. Neither the waitress nor the grubby-looking men at the corner table seemed to care. A nasal-voiced man was singing on the tinny radio in Russian and English: *"Ahn-gel, moi ahn-gel, dooo it to me now."*

"But remember, you can't tell your mama that I told you. Can you keep a secret?"

Tanya ticked off secrets in her head: Mama's story about Papa's death, Daddy's story about finding Mama, Babushka's warning about the photograph. She nodded vigorously.

"So." Liuba dabbed her lips with a napkin. "Your mama and papa were very romantic, always fighting and making up. Aunt Galya would come over to our place crying, complaining that your papa spent too much time drinking with his friends, especially after you were born. She used to argue with him, and sometimes he hit her."

"Papa hit Mama?" Her mother had warned her about Liuba: she was a lying know-it-all. But, Tanya wondered, could a person really be both?

"Yeah. He would knock her around a little bit, but then he'd give her flowers and they'd be in love again. By the way, I don't think you should interrupt me. You can ask me questions later." Liuba took a sip of mango nectar and smacked her lips. "So your mama had a friend who found out about a company that helped women get American husbands. And one day, when she was really mad at your papa, your mama signed up."

"But—" Liuba shot her a look. *But Mama already had a husband,* Tanya wanted to say. Instead, she ate the last bite of her caviar sandwich. The dried-out eggs pasted the roof of her mouth like fishy peanut butter.

"She said she wanted to make your papa jealous," Liuba said. "But she was scared to tell him about it at first." Galina received dozens of letters from lonely American men. She'd bring them over for Liuba to translate.

Liuba knew English? Tanya had never heard her speak a word of it.

" 'All he wants is a maid,' Aunt Galya would say." Liuba's voice turned high and girlish when she quoted Tanya's mother. " 'Who would marry him?' But there was one guy she thought was OK. They started writing back and forth. His letters were really boring, all about his job working with computers, the history of California, but your mama, she didn't mind." Liuba gazed dreamily out the door. One day, she said, the American wrote to say that he wanted to visit. Galina told Tanya's papa. "She made him jealous, all right." Liuba narrowed her eyes. "They had a big fight, and he gave her a black eye."

The men in the corner erupted in laughter. Tanya jumped.

"You and your mama lived with us after that," Liuba said. "And she began to think maybe it wasn't such a crazy idea, marrying an American." The American arrived in Petrozavodsk and checked into a hotel; he rented a neighbor's car and went on drives with Galina. Sometimes they took Tanya with them, but on the day they took the boat to Kizhi, they left her behind. "Galina was sure he was going to propose to her there, but he didn't." Liuba had slipped into a reverie; her green eyes sent off yellow sparks. "Galya said she wasn't sure she wanted to marry him, anyway. Because of your papa. 'I can't imagine never seeing him again'—that's exactly what she said."

One night during the American's visit, Liuba said, Tanya's papa came by the apartment. They could tell he'd been drinking. Galina told him that he was a terrible husband and father and that if he didn't stop drinking immediately, she and the American would get married and take Tanya to California. She said all of this in a polite voice, so the American wouldn't catch on. Tanya's papa left without saying a word. "The American started asking questions," Liuba said. "Galya told him that the man was her ex-husband, as if she were already divorced. I heard her crying in her room that night."

The syrupy smell of mango nectar rose from the cup; Tanya drank it down in one gulp.

"Like I said, the American was using our neighbor's car, and he kept it parked in the guy's garage. In the morning, when Galya and the American opened up the garage, they found your papa inside the car. He was dead. He must have known the American was using the car. He broke in and turned on the gas, and that's how he died." Liuba stared coolly at Tanya. "Your papa, he wasn't anything like mine. My papa was a war hero. Your papa killed himself."

Tanya thought of the man in the photo, his taut muscles, the look he had given the camera, a mixture of defiance and tenderness. "But Papa worked at the ice-cream factory," she said.

"Sure, he worked there," Liuba said. "But he killed himself

in a car." The American went home the next day, and they all went to the funeral. The scandal spread quickly. Galina cried for weeks and rarely left the house. She wrote letters to the American, which Liuba took to the post office. "She thought she might as well try to give you a nice life. But for a long time, the American didn't write back."

Tanya knew how the real story ended: she and her mother moved to America. They lived with her daddy in a house in San Francisco. Liuba would tell it wrong, and Tanya would know it had all been a lie.

"Finally, though, he sent Galya a letter. He told her that in spite of everything, he loved her, and he loved you, too. He wanted to marry her and be your new father." Liuba shrugged. "You and your mama moved to America. That's about it."

Tanya looked down at her stomach and was surprised it looked just as it always did. For as Liuba spoke, something had grown within Tanya, a block of coldness, foreign and hard, numbing her from the inside out.

At home, incense hung in the hallway like a fine mist.

"Babushka!" Liuba shouted, tripping over Tanya on the threshold. Since they'd left the bar, Tanya felt as if she were a toy soldier, her legs and arms stiff as wood. Liuba ran into Babushka's room and began to wail.

"Mama!" Tanya cried. She flung her arms around Galina's waist and let herself be carried to the kitchen table. Burying her head in her mother's shoulder, she began to sob.

"Tanichka, darling." Galina cradled Tanya in her lap like a baby and smoothed her hair. "Don't worry, she's still with us. There's still time to say good-bye." Her eyes shone with excitement. "The priest was just here," she whispered. "It's happening so fast, Tanya, just like the doctor said!"

"Mama . . ." Tanya needed to explain: she was not crying

because of Babushka. "Papa," she choked. From the bedroom, Liuba wailed on and on.

"That's right, honey, we'll go home to Papa soon." Galina beamed. "After the funeral, we'll go straight back to San Francisco. In just a few days, you'll see."

Had Mama forgotten about Papa? Tanya's sobs ended in a great gulp of air. She leaned back to study her mother. Galina's hair was pulled into a loose bun; her skin glowed as pink and fuzzy as a peach. Lips slightly parted, she averted her eyes from Tanya's gaze. It was the same expression she wore at home when she brought supper to the table or accepted a kiss from Daddy—a still, quiet look, as if she were listening to distant music. She was a beauty; everyone said so. But until today Galina had been no one to Tanya but her mother.

"Where'd you learn to stare like that, Tanya?" Galina said. "You're giving me the chills."

"What was his name?" Tanya asked.

Her mother shook her head. "Whose name?"

"Papa. What was Papa's name?"

"You mean your Russian papa?"

Tanya nodded.

Galina frowned at Tanya for a long moment, then lowered her to the ground. "Liuba!" Galina marched across the hallway. "Liubov Osipovna Plevitskaya!" Liuba's wails broke off abruptly. Tanya heard a rush of footsteps behind Babushka's door, then the turn of the lock. Galina rattled the knob. "You can't hide in there forever." She slumped against the door.

"What did she tell you?" Galina said after gathering Tanya up and settling her on their bed with the door closed.

Tanya took out the photograph. Galina studied it, a film slowly forming on her eyes. She set the photo aside and enfolded Tanya, lowering them both to the pillow. "You don't know what it's like for me, being here," Galina whispered. "It's like being back in prison after having escaped."

"Mama. You and Daddy didn't get married at Kizhi. Did you?"

Galina lay very still. After a minute, Tanya worried that her mother was falling asleep. Finally she spoke, her breath warm in Tanya's ear. "My little girl's growing up. She's getting too old for make-believe."

"No I'm not." Tanya pulled her mother's arms tighter around her.

Galina sighed. "Nobody really lives at Kizhi, Tanya, and nobody gets married there. But it's fun to pretend, isn't it?"

Tanya thought of the coin in her purse. "Yes," she said.

Galina's arms loosened, and Tanya turned to face her. "Daddy's such a good man," Galina said. "He pays the phone bill every month, never a day late. Can you imagine that? When you grow up, he'll put you through college. Isn't that wonderful?"

"Mama," Tanya said.

"His name was Dmitri. Dmitri Stepanovich Orlov." Galina fingered the sleeve of Tanya's T-shirt. "So your given name was Tatiana Dmitrievna Orlova." Galina sat up, and Tanya tried to get up with her, but her mother edged her down. "You rest. Tomorrow will be a long day. I'll make sure you see your grandmother before she goes."

The light that seeped through the lacy curtains was like a magic dye that made the armchair, the dresser, everything in the room glow pink from the inside. Tanya's mother slept soundly beside her; the apartment was hushed. Was it day or night?

Tanya tiptoed into her grandmother's room. Someone had taken the blankets down from the windows. Babushka's eyes were shut, her hands folded neatly on the coverlet. Her skin was the color of bone. Her wrist, when Tanya touched it, felt cool, as if she had been standing outside on a chilly day.

Tanya settled onto the bedside chair, feeling ashamed that she hadn't said good-bye, ashamed she felt so relieved. Her gaze drifted outside, to the courtyard. Three garages were scattered at odd angles across the dirt yard. A Russian garage was not like an American garage; it was not a little house. A Russian garage folded snugly over a car like a rolltop desk. Tanya went to the window and pressed her fingers to the cold glass. She wondered how someone could have shut himself inside.

"My Tanichka's come for her lesson."

Tanya turned, stifling a scream. Babushka's dark eyes were open, and her hand reached out. Blinking back tears, Tanya returned to the bed and clasped the brittle fingers.

"We'll study tomorrow, all right?" Babushka said. "I'm not feeling so well today."

"All right," Tanya said.

"My American granddaughter." Babushka gargled a laugh. "Who would've thought?" Her grip tightened. "But Russian, too. Russian first of all."

"Russian first of all," Tanya whispered.

A cry came from the courtyard. A stout old woman in an apron and a little boy had appeared and were playing badminton in a far corner of the square. The boy staggered backward, and his racket arced through the air. The old woman gave a whoop, and the birdie vanished into the pale pink sky.

The sun was a low wedge of orange sliced by bars of iron clouds; just beneath, feathery white waves crested from the dark water. In the middle of the lakeside field, Tanya balanced on tiptoe, hands braced against the tree statue's black trunk. *Whisper one wish.* Her lips grazed the bottom of the big white ear, then slipped lower as she lost her footing. Bells chimed from the highest limbs. Or was it voices Tanya heard?

Voices, blooming into English: "Oh, the sweet thing's not

tall enough." Four women in pastel pants and jackets, their hair cotton-candy puffs, regarded Tanya from the path. "Do you speak any English, little girl?" one of them asked.

Tanya nodded.

"Well, bless your heart. Here, let me give you a boost. We made our wishes yesterday, on our tour. Maybe mine'll come true if I help you."

The woman's hands were warm and strong. Tanya cupped the ear and nuzzled its cold hollow. "Tree," she whispered in Russian, "please make sure that Babushka dies soon so that Mama and I can go home to Daddy, and also please tell Papa that I miss him."

"Thank you very much," Tanya said after the woman had set her down.

"My, you speak beautiful English!" the woman cried.

Tanya nodded. Her voice had impressed her as well. After all, she hadn't spoken English since her telephone conversation with her father, which seemed like ages ago, a memory from earliest childhood.

Tanya followed the women down the boardwalk. "Ahoy there, lassies!" an old man called in English from the boat's railing. Three other old men stood beside him, jaunty in white caps and shoes. The women waved and hooted. Tanya watched from the dock as they fussed with tickets and stepped cautiously onto the gangplank.

"Are you going to Kizhi, young lady?" a man said in Russian.

Tanya turned. A stooped old man with a fishing pole slung over his shoulder was smiling at her. She stared until she recognized him. It was the ice-cream man. Outside of his kiosk, he looked small and frail. The edges of his brown suit shone like polished shoes.

"I don't have a ticket," Tanya said.

"Do you want to go?"

She hesitated. "With you?"

"Sure, why not?"

Tanya didn't need to worry anymore about seeing the church where her parents had not, after all, been married. But it would please Daddy to know that she'd been there, and it would be nice to be able to describe it to him in her own words. "All right," she said.

The old man patted his pockets. "Only, I don't seem to be carrying my wallet today." Tanya emptied her change purse into his chapped palm. He shook his fist in the air. "I'll be right back!"

The American women stood at the boat's railing, laughing with their husbands. Tanya would burrow among them, surrounding herself with their soft bodies, soothing colors, and familiar voices. Then she'd stare at the horizon and wait. First the domes of the wooden church would appear, then the spires and roofs of the other buildings, the village gathering before her like something that had been there all along, like something that always would be.

HONEY MONTH

Jack could not leave Russia today. That was the verdict of the fifth and final immigration official, delivered as his gaze flipped from Jack to Rachel—from withering contempt to withering pity—outside his office in a grimy corner of Sheremetevo Airport. To be perfectly clear: there was absolutely no possibility of a foreigner exiting Moscow on a student visa that had expired three months ago. Jack would have to go back into town, visit this acronymed office and that one. There would be stamps to collect, fines to pay, documents to *vozobnovit'*.

As her mind snagged on the unfamiliar verb, Rachel turned her attention from the official's words to his appearance. She had noticed the wedding band right away—a flashy accessory for a Russian man. He wore an olive-green uniform; an invisible hat had caused his hair to dampen and set in waves. One of his epaulets, missing its red-star button, was held in place by a safety pin. Rachel imagined a wife too sloppy and thick-fingered to handle a needle and thread. She saw the official stripped down to boxers, a plastic-billed cap restored to his head, his sweaty wife busting out of her slip, sucking on his earlobe. Newlyweds, both long divorced, drunk on unexpected midlife passion.

As if confirming her vision, the official jerked his head at Rachel, a smile twitching at his mouth.

"Myedovii myesyats," Rachel breathed, pointing from her to Jack. Honey month, she translated to herself. She was sure she'd found the official's soft spot, and it was only a fib—they were *supposed* to be going on their honeymoon.

The official snorted and took a step back, absorbing Rachel and Jack in one gaze instead of two. Linking herself more closely to Jack had been a miscalculation, she realized. Should she start crying? But tears, even real ones, never seemed to have any effect in this country, and anyway, it was too late; the official was returning Jack's expired visa with a slap to the palm. Clicking his heels, he spun around and vanished behind the cardboard door of his office.

"Nu, nichevo," Jack muttered, gazing at the loose strip of wood-grain contact paper that fluttered in the bureaucrat's wake. *"Nado prosto vernut'sya v tsentr, i—"*

"Po-angliskii, mozhno?" Rachel interrupted. Shall we try English? Jack spoke and read Russian all day long; he even thought in Russian now. But they were both American. What had happened to the internal switch that flipped his brain back to English at the sight of her? Lately, it had been short-circuiting.

Jack revolved stiffly, his face hooded in mid-flinch. *"Mozhno,"* he agreed.

"Jack?" Tiny daggers pricked up and down Rachel's throat; now that the official was gone, useless tears threatened. "How did this happen?"

"Those guys in Helsinki screwed me." Shaking his head, Jack launched into the theory he'd developed during their hour-long dash through the airport. Corrupt officials at the Russian embassy in Finland were responsible for him unwittingly overstaying his welcome in Russia, he insisted. "I'm *sure* I paid for a six-month visa. I knew that red-haired woman was no good."

As he rambled, Rachel's eyes welled; Jack swam into soft focus. She had gotten a new visa during a trip home to Chicago the previous summer, a trip Jack had forgone in favor of Helsinki—closer, cheaper, faster. Had he never looked at the expiration date on his visa? Or had he gambled on the benevolence of airport bureaucrats and lost? He did at least give the *appearance* of someone who expected to leave Russia for a slightly warmer climate: clean-shaven, overcoat instead of down parka, knees poking through the holes in his jeans. Of course he didn't want to stay here; of course he wasn't to blame. What kind of man would deliberately blow off his honeymoon? A Russo-Finnish shakedown was more plausible, though it was true Jack had blown off their wedding. Which wasn't entirely his fault, either. Rachel should have predicted that, absorbed by his dissertation research at the archive, he would never get around to finding out how two Americans might have their union sanctified by the Russian government. Her crumb of complicity brought her some relief.

"The twelve-month was too expensive," he was saying, "but I had enough for the six-month. I'm sure it was the six-month . . ." He frowned. "Unless . . ."

"Jack?" Rachel said. "The flight. It's soon. Do you want me to stay here with you?"

"Oh." The hoods lowered over his eyes, rendering him inscrutable. "Do you *want* to stay?"

Rachel thought of the sticky seats and exhaust fumes of the bus back to Moscow, of the slush they would plow through as they scavenged one government stamp after another. It was late January; the holidays had finally ended, and drunkenness and despondency hung over Moscow like a black dome. Just the other night on the subway, everyone—a bickering couple, a weeping woman, eight or nine doubled-over men of all ages—*everyone* was drunk, including Jack and Rachel, slumped against each other on the bench. What if they couldn't get to Prague tonight? She thought of their apartment, the air heavy with the grease of last night's fried chicken, the armchair heaped with ancient laundry waiting to be cranked in the oversized salad spinner that hooked up to the tub. For months, the promise of ten days outside Russia had begun to feel to Rachel like a narrow escape from some unknown but inevitable disaster—no more so than at this moment.

"You'll get there tonight?" she said.

"Tonight. Tomorrow morning at the latest." He held up two fingers—scout's honor. Had he ever been a Boy Scout? She couldn't remember.

"I might as well go, then." She tried to sound blasé. "Stake out the best beds at the hostel."

The hoods slid up, and one of Jack's almost extinct American smiles—open, guileless—bloomed. "I guess we'd better run," he said.

As they crossed the concourse back to customs, bleary, sweat-smeared faces passed in and out of the cones of smoky light leaking from the ceiling's tin-can fixtures. Sheremetevo Airport always reminded Rachel of a seedy nightclub. A synthetic pop song thudded from the airport café, where two leathery men faced off like gunslingers over a high table, tossing back single-serving plastic containers of vodka.

Customs was a mosh pit, seething and roiling; they edged to its perimeter and were quickly repelled. Jack slung the duffel bag onto Rachel's shoulder and instructed her to call him from Prague. "I'll get it all straightened out at OVIR," he shouted above the drum-machine beat. "Like the guy said, it'll be a piece of cake."

The official had said nothing about cake, Rachel was certain, or its idiomatic equivalent, as if there could be one, as if anything were ever simple here. *Khotelos' kak luchshe, a poluchilos' kak vsegda.* It was one of the few Russian expressions she'd absorbed by osmosis, so often had she heard it uttered by their friends, the secretaries at work, politicians on TV, and now it mockingly insinuated itself: We hoped for the best, but things turned out as they always do.

"Hey, sweetie." Jack's fingertips flicked over her cheek, as if testing an iron's heat. "Forgive me?"

She opened her mouth to say something—what, she had no idea—but Jack cut her off, zooming in with a dry kiss, his lips jutting and pecking like a beak. He nudged her into the throng; a suitcase hit her in the shin, and she shoved back with equal force. "See you soon!" she heard him calling.

When she turned, he was gone.

Aboard the plane, Russians and Czechs, sucking down cigarettes, squeezed steamer trunks and bulging plaid duffels into overhead bins. Beyond the tarmac, candy wrappers and empty bottles glinted on a field of soot-encrusted snow. A line of spindly birch trees shivered on the horizon. When they descended into Moscow eighteen months ago, Jack had pointed out those very trees as if he had planted them for her. "Welcome to Russia," he said.

Averting her eyes, Rachel found herself staring at another line of trees, this one stamped against the bulkhead burlap in orange paint, haloed by a stylized umber sunset, or maybe a mustard smear. She rummaged through her backpack for her book, the only English-language reading material in their apartment she hadn't read twice, or even once: the autobiography of Nina Berberova, wife of Vladislav Khodasevich, the poet Jack had come to Russia to study. Rachel had started it soon after she and Jack agreed to marry, smugly imagining the displaced intellectuals to be kindred spirits. But through the long winter months when Jack mentioned neither marriage nor returning home, she hadn't had the heart to look at it.

She steeled herself. It was 1921, St. Petersburg was in chaos, and Berberova was falling in love:

There was an evening, clear and starlit, when the snow crackled and sparkled: both of us—Khodasevich and I— hurried past the Mikhailovsky Theatre, and in the square for some reason searchlights had been installed; in their rays our breath hung in wreaths.

Rachel thought of the snowy night she first crossed Red Square with Jack, more than a year ago; in the floodlights of St. Basil's, snow fell like chains of pearls against a black-velvet backdrop. The memory might have been as perfect as Berberova's if Rachel hadn't handed over her new Nikon to the cheerful young man who volunteered to take their picture. Jack chased the thief three times around GUM, returning with empty hands and a pained expression. "Let's not mention this to anyone, OK?" he said, explaining that Russians tended to think Americans were careless with money. Rachel realized he was worried about his new friends, the malnourished graduate students he unearthed in the stacks of the archive. Not that he blamed Rachel, he insisted. But people might jump to the wrong conclusion.

A week later, when one of Jack's friends asked Rachel over the crowded dinner table about her monthly salary, she blurted out the paltry sum her multinational employer paid her to su- pervise the Russian secretaries, and she was amused by the rev- erent hush that followed. That night in bed, Jack fretted that his friends would resent them now.

It took her aback: Jack was ashamed of her. He thought she was too American. When she agreed to join him in Russia for his fellowship year, Rachel had expected to struggle more with herself than with him—for having nothing better to do than to follow her boyfriend abroad. She hadn't considered that her gullibility, her frankness when others might hedge, her braying laugh—qualities that had pleased him during their two years together in Chicago—would, in Moscow, make him stammer and cringe.

She found excuses for him. Wasn't it his sympathetic melancholia for the suffering of the Russian people that had first attracted her during that temp gig in Slavic studies? Even Jack's crusade to restore poor, neglected Khodasevich to literary prominence showed the depths of his cultural sensitivity.

She toned down her laugh, hid her bourgeois provisions from their friends (the toilet-paper roll she carried in her backpack, the *People* magazines her mother sent from home), and avoided speaking Russian in Jack's presence—which wasn't easy in Moscow. She blended in, and in the process felt some core part of herself dilute, replaced by a new resilience, a tolerance for indignity. What rattled her in the early months didn't touch her anymore: not the jostling, the staring, the pools of melted slush on shop floors; not the disappearance of her parents and friends from daily life; not the steely-eyed saleswomen or her French boss, screaming about tardy secretaries; not even the legless man who swept their courtyard every morning on a wheeled cart, rowing himself with his broom of twigs.

It would only be a year. Back home, she and Jack would be on equal footing again, and she might flourish in some unforeseen way that would delight them both.

All through summer, she mentioned return tickets, but Jack shrugged her off until a night in late August. They were playing their usual game of rummy at the kitchen table, the windows thrown wide open against the heat, the radio tuned to pop hits, Elton John and Alla Pugachova. He wasn't ready, Jack told her. To write a good dissertation, he would need another year of research. She could stand another year here, couldn't she? It wasn't as if she knew what she wanted to do back home, right?

She started to cry, and to berate him for his habit of speaking of their life in the States as something odious but unavoidable, like repayment of his college loans.

What if they got married, he said, tossing the proposal onto the table as casually as he would a trio of aces. Not at home, as they'd discussed, but here in Moscow. A trial commitment before the real thing.

It was a bribe—she knew that. Maybe that was why she accepted so quickly, for fear they would consider the offer too closely and miss their chance at happiness. They threw a small party, drank too much to their good fortune, and when they decided to renew their visas in Prague, Rachel suggested that they think of the trip as a honeymoon. Jack agreed, and he also agreed that no one at home needed to know their plans. Their families might feel excluded, Rachel reasoned, or worry that they would never come home. She didn't mention what her mother said when Rachel told her they were staying another year: "I know this is important to Jack, honey, but what about *your* plans?" Aside from staying with Jack, Rachel didn't have any plans. In Moscow, she had taken the admissions test for American graduate schools, but only to keep her options open. Each day for months, it seemed, Jack failed to stop by ZAGS to inquire about expatriate weddings, and each night he failed to mention the lapse. Meanwhile, their Russian friends teased them about their honeymoon in Prague.

The jets were howling; cigarette smoke hovered in the air like chalk dust. A flight attendant swiveled down the aisle, snapping the bins shut with French-tipped fingers. The plane rumbled down the runway and lifted heavily from the ground. Rachel closed her eyes. She felt the plane duck once, as if reconsidering, then soar bravely skyward.

It was the Russians who dressed up for the flight, the women in ruffled blouses and chunky heels, the men in tweedy caps and three-piece suits that looked cut from the same pilling bolt of rayon. But at the Prague airport, the Russians and their red passports were picked off one by one and ushered behind a winding line of African students in bright parkas, while Rachel and the Czechs, in their jeans and slouchy sweaters, breezed through to baggage claim. Now she stood staring fixedly with the Czechs at the mouth of the carousel, as if their collective will would inspire the blue light to flash, the suitcases to begin chugging down.

A pinging sound came from overhead, like rain on sheet metal, growing louder. It approached the chute, then the carousel, like machine-gun fire.

Little bottles came raining down, little plastic jars, some disappearing into the crevices of the carousel, others bursting on impact with its outer lip, spraying hard bits of something—candy or pills, white and tan and orange—into the air.

The Czechs gasped and jumped back. Rachel did too.

A scuffed black slipper slid down the chute, followed by a navy-blue T-shirt and a tube of toothpaste. Two more bottles shot down, popping their caps.

Tablets scattered at Rachel's feet. Large, oblong ones that would burn the throat. The Czechs murmured to each other and backed away, kicking pills from their path.

When the slipper made its second revolution, Rachel grabbed it, then started digging pill bottles out of the carousel's cracks. She plucked up the T-shirt and a pair of khaki pants that had slithered down and formed a pile at her feet, ignoring the uniform expression, bemused disdain, on the faces of the Czechs nearby.

"*Bozhe moi!*" A young woman was scuffing up to the carousel. "*Spasibo, dyevushka, spasibo,*" she murmured to Rachel. Thank you, young lady.

"*Nichevo,*" Rachel said, blushing, and lunged for a pink bathrobe.

"Good God, if my husband sees this . . ." The woman pressed her hand to her forehead as she surveyed the pile. She looked to be in her early thirties, dressed in a loose white blouse and stirrup pants, light brown hair pulled into a high ponytail. Before Rachel learned how common the woman's fine-boned beauty was in Russia, she would have mistaken her for a former ballerina or figure skater.

Another pair of khaki pants and another navy shirt tumbled down, and Rachel and the woman sprang into action. Working as a team, they salvaged bras and briefs, a chunky hairbrush, a travel-sized bottle of hair spray. The flow slowed to a trickle, and the suitcase appeared, tumbling end over end, gaping and empty.

Rachel was folding a shirt, and the woman was tucking toiletries into the case when a man stomped up to them, growling Russian-inflected phrases. Curses, probably. Rachel didn't know any; Jack's friends thought swearing uncouth, and the prissy Pioneer children in the Soviet text her office tutor used never sunk to foul language as they tsk-tsked over America's oppression of its native people and former slaves. "Mother," she picked out of the man's spit-laden torrent, and "pierogi," and a word she thought meant "horns."

His skin was an angry red; rivulets of sweat trickled from crew cut to brow. He looked like the bodyguards who muscled through the line at the Prospect Mira McDonald's, cell phone to ear, barking out their bosses' orders to the quaking teenagers behind the counter. But instead of a counterfeit Adidas jogging suit, the man wore a navy polo shirt and khaki pants, identical to the outfits Rachel had been folding. She glimpsed a green embroidered alligator on the navy-blue windbreaker he was wringing in his fists. Rachel stared. She had never seen a Russian preppie before.

"What's going on here?" he said, miraculously breaking into first-year Russian.

"It must have broken on the plane," the woman said.

Whipping his jacket to the ground, the man seized the suitcase and jiggled the clasp. "Kaput!" he confirmed, and let loose a few stray curses. He throttled the suitcase and flung it down, then squinted at Rachel. "Do you work here?"

"Yegor," the woman said, raising her eyebrows, "this young lady has been helping us."

"Helping?" Yegor frowned at the woman. "Why?"

"She's just being kind, I think." Doubt filled the woman's eyes.

Yegor flashed his traveling companion a look of panicked dismay, the same look Jack had given Rachel when she held out her camera to the thief on Red Square.

"Yes," Rachel said, annoyed.

Yegor's eyes narrowed. "What are you, American?"

Did she really say "*Da*" with an accent? Or did her assistance betray uniquely American luxuries—an excess of time and naïveté? Jack would be mortified if he were here, she thought, and for the first time she felt glad he wasn't. "*Da*," she sighed.

"This suitcase is American," Yegor said, giving it a kick. His suspicions gone, he seemed manic, almost merry. "Three hundred bucks at GUM. These vitamins are American, too." His foot swabbed the area in front of him, rattling pills across the tile.

Mercifully, Rachel's duffel bag glided by. She chased after it, planning to sneak away to a cab. But when she turned from the carousel, the couple blocked her way. The other passengers had dispersed, she noted, except for a couple of teenagers snickering at them from a distance. "Excuse me, *dyevushka*, but we were wondering," the woman said, "are you traveling alone?"

Rachel nodded, then shook her head. "My boyfriend—my fiancé—he's coming . . . soon."

"Your fiancé lets you travel alone?" Yegor said.

The absurd question loosened something in Rachel. She swallowed, working at the dumpling that had lodged in her throat. As the couple looked on, she fumbled through her backpack, pulled out her stash of toilet paper, and began sniffling into the tail end. The roll slipped from her grasp and unwound, the tan crepe paper gathering in loops at her feet.

"There, there," the woman cooed as she balled up the streamers.

"Fuck," Rachel muttered.

Yegor let out a laugh. "Fuck," he parroted, and Rachel found herself smiling encouragingly, pleased to have stumbled upon the one English word that would charm him. Yegor jumped in with introductions. He was Yegor, and Lena was his wife.

"Rachel," Rachel said, hand over heart.

"Listen, *dyevushka*, where are you staying?" Yegor demanded.

What was Russian for hostel? "Gostel?" she transliterated, wiping her eyes, thinking of Gerbalife, Planet Gollywood, German Gesse, but they didn't understand until she had pulled out her Prague guidebook and Yegor underlined "US$7/night" with a meaty thumb. He made a hissing sound.

"Rachel, come with us," Lena said. "We're staying at a nice, safe hotel, right in the center—very affordable. At least until your fiancé gets here."

"I don't know . . ." Rachel said. It had been Jack's idea to stay in a hostel, and she had agreed, knowing how small his stipend was, regretting her disloyal thought: Leave it to us to spend our honeymoon in a youth hostel. But Yegor was already hoisting Rachel's duffel bag over his shoulder, and she felt cheered by the prospect of guides into the city and an accommodation upgrade. She grabbed her backpack and trotted after them. She hoped they were staying at a five-star hotel. She hadn't used her credit card in months.

Answering a knock at her door the next morning, Rachel tried
to hide her disappointment when she found Lena, not Jack, on
the other side. Yegor had gone off on business, Lena told her;
would she be interested in sight-seeing? Lena was an architect
who had studied in Prague, and she wanted to show off some
of her favorite buildings. Rachel had been dreading the day—
alone and adrift in a strange city—and quickly accepted.

Out on the street, a gauze curtain of fog enveloped the
stucco buildings of the tourist district. On the bus into town,
they had passed rows of dingy white housing blocks, and the
subway cars were Soviet, too, but the city center had sloughed
off all imprints of Russia. Compared to the frenetic Muscovites
Rachel was used to, the Czechs she and Lena passed on
Wenceslas Square looked stoned.

It was a point in Lena's favor that, as they followed a snaking
alleyway to Old Town Square, she didn't inquire further about
Jack's absence. Rachel had called him the night before from a
booth in the telegraph office—one couldn't make long-
distance calls from the hotel. The woman at the front counter
dialed Jack's cell phone, and soon Rachel heard the mournful
falsetto of the old woman who hawked fried chicken in their
neighborhood square. He had waited at the visa office all afternoon, he told her, and as soon as he got to the front of the line,
they shut the window. He would go back in the morning
and—hopefully, he said—see her later in the day, today.

As they strolled, Lena pointed at buildings, one century
lined up against the next, her lecture on cornices and mosaics
spliced with asides about men setting themselves on fire, tanks
rolling in and out of the city, ghetto walls rising and crumbling.
Rachel relaxed, her anxiety about Jack dissipating beside the
heft of European history. When Lena fell silent, Rachel began
to prattle ungrammatically about Jack's violation of Russia's visa
regulations and his entrapment in Moscow, using whatever
motion verbs and case endings popped into her head. Lena's

gasps of shock and sympathy spurred Rachel on to the punch line: this was supposed to be, but wasn't their "honey month."

"*Koshmar*," Lena murmured—what a nightmare—and latched onto Rachel's arm. Rachel, who had always envied the physical closeness between Russian women, felt so grateful for the gesture that she grew newly shy.

They crossed Charles Bridge and took a tram up to the castle. No longer entwined, but side by side, they squinted up at the massive stone cathedral posed against a blinding gray sky. Jagged and somber, coated in a black moss of soot, the cathedral looked ugly to Rachel. She had grown used to squat stucco churches with roly-poly domes like swirling marbles.

"Last year I designed a church," Lena said. "A *kapella*, I should say." Her hands sculpted an onion in the air. "Tiny, tiny—just one dome." A chapel, Rachel thought. "It was part of a luxury complex on the highway. Every time I visited, I imagined a New Russian standing in it, trying to call God on his cell phone."

Rachel laughed but felt distressed, remembering the last church she visited, at a monastery outside Moscow. It was a cool, sunny day, and she and an American woman from her office sat down on a bench to admire the church's pristine white-washed walls, the true-blue domes flecked with gold stars, like a child's art project. On the next bench, an old woman began to rage: they had no right to be there; they were intruding; why didn't they go back where they came from? Another woman scolded her for harassing the foreigners, who after all were doing no harm. As the two women quarreled, Rachel and Beth Ann slunk away.

"My boyfriend doesn't think tourists should visit churches," Rachel said now.

"It's good he's not here, then," Lena said, grinning at her sidelong.

Caught off guard, Rachel laughed. "Maybe so."

"It's funny that you're here for a Russian visa," Lena said. "We're here for an American one." She had been granted a tourist visa in Moscow, she explained, but Yegor had been turned down. "It's a long shot, but we thought we'd try again here. He's at your embassy right now."

"You're moving to America?" Rachel asked. Their desire to be in each other's countries hung between them, embarassing and sad, as if the four of them were misfits who, full of false hope, expected to fit in elsewhere. Yegor had said he was a *biz-nesmen*, a real estate developer specializing in *pavilioni* and *mini-marti*. The U.S. embassy bureaucrats must not have been persuaded that he had anything worth returning to in Moscow. Were Yegor's preppie outfits modeled on the business-casual wardrobes he'd spotted at the American embassy? Rachel felt ashamed. Unlike Jack, Yegor hadn't broken any regulations, but her government considered him undesirable.

"Just visiting." Lena unbuttoned her coat and smoothed her hand over her blouse, revealing a small bulge. "We're going to America to have the baby."

"Oh!" Rachel said, startled. "Congratulations!"

"Thanks." Lena smiled. "I'm just a few months along. That's why all the vitamins—Yegor insists. And he wants the baby to have U.S. citizenship."

"That's possible? Go there, have the baby, then leave?"

"Any baby born in America is automatically an American citizen," Lena said.

There were other questions Rachel wanted to ask, but following her new friend's example, she didn't pry. "I hope it works out," she said. "The visa, I mean."

"And for Jack, too," said Lena.

"Oh, it'll be fine. Probably he'll be at the hotel when we get back."

Lena's expression was searching, but ended with a nod. She linked arms with Rachel again and steered her around the cathedral and down a cobbled path. Rachel pressed close to Lena for warmth as they poked their heads into former homes, now shops—one of them Kafka's, the doorframe tiled with postcards—built into the castle walls.

Rachel's first Russian friend, and Jack didn't even know her.

The hotel was an Art Nouveau showcase, standing in the middle of Wenceslas Square like a tarnished trophy on a mantel. Jack wasn't in the lobby or outside Rachel's door. No message at the front desk, either. At the telegraph office around the corner, the middle-aged woman behind the pane of glass dialed Jack's cell phone while Rachel listened to the archaic beeps and squawks from what had begun to feel like her booth.

He was at their apartment. He'd collected his stamps and documents and was free to go, but he hadn't made it to the airport yet. "I had to wrap up some stuff, and I lost track of time," he said. "I'd better wait until morning."

"What stuff?"

"I mean, if you still think I should come."

"What? Jack, this is our—" She stopped herself.

"Listen, Rach. What if once I'm there, the Russians won't give me a new visa? What if they won't let me back in because I overstayed?"

"They wouldn't do that. Anyway, you have to leave. They're onto you now, right?"

"I'm just saying—"

"What are you doing there, anyway?"

"Nastya needed some help with a translation. She just left."

Nastya, the Bulgakov expert, a twenty-year-old divorcée with stork legs and a cherub's face. Rachel trusted Jack, but a girl named Nastya? "You know, Jack," she blurted, "you can't stay in Russia forever."

"I'll be there tomorrow," he said grimly.

At the window, the clerk pushed a pile of crowns through the hole; they had both expected her call to Russia to last longer. On impulse, Rachel slid the money back, added a few more bills, and passed the woman a second number.

"Hello?" Rachel's mother answered the phone in her morning voice, sleepy and low.

Rachel held the receiver away from her mouth. She didn't know what to say.

"Rachel, is that you?" her mother said. "Honey, if it's you, call me back. We've got a bad connection again. I think you're on your trip—Prague, was it? Anyway, honey, call me back if it's you. I miss you, cutie. Hope everything's OK."

She fell silent, but Rachel could still hear her breathing. Rachel pressed the receiver close and waited until her mother hung up.

Rachel's hotel room was a garret, the kind the orphaned heroines of her favorite books from childhood had lived in. She ate dinner, cookies and apple juice, at the small desk by the double-paned window. The bed was a single, the mattress thin as a yoga mat, a rust-stained sink beside it. Without thinking, she had asked for a room for one, then failed to correct herself, reasoning that the hotel was dead, and they would have no trouble switching to a double when Jack arrived.

Lena knocked on the door and called her name; Rachel held still and waited for the two sets of footsteps to pass. She climbed into bed with her book. Facing persecution, Berberova and Khodasevich fled Russia and alighted in one European city after another, finally settling in Paris, where the poet fell into despair at the thought of never seeing Russia again.

Khodasevich, exhausted by insomnia, could not find a place for himself: "Here I cannot, cannot, I cannot live and write, *there* I cannot, cannot live and write." I saw how, in those moments, he was building up his own personal or private hell around himself and how he pulled me into that hell; and I trustingly followed him . . .

When Rachel turned out the light, the room felt like a Russian train car—it was about the same size and shape. The last time she and Jack took an overnight train to St. Petersburg, they had ridden *platzkart*, sleeping in the open bunks to save money; at bedtime, he reached to squeeze her hand in the space between their upper berths. Now, in her mind, she saw herself and Jack as two figures on stained glass, fists clasped. As the colors on the glass seeped away, she erased the image, fearing the moment when the figures would be linked by nothing but a black outline, thick and leaden.

In the hotel's café the next morning, Lena and Yegor flagged Rachel to their table by the picture window.

"So, Rachel, tell me," Yegor said as she settled into the seat next to Lena. "Is it customary in America for the bride to spend her entire honeymoon alone?"

"Stop," Lena scolded, and began commenting on the room's carved paneling, the light fixtures strung with beads. Rachel stared past the lace swags that framed the quiet promenade, where a middle-aged man and woman in orange vests sat smoking on a bench, garbage tongs at their sides.

"Before the wedding?" Yegor added.

"*Myedovii myesyats,*" Rachel muttered, glaring at him. "Why is it called honey month in Russian, anyway? People don't go away for a month."

"Not month, Rachel," Lena said gently. "*Myesyats* has another meaning: a partial *luna*."

"Moon? You say honeymoon, too?" Only after Rachel argued that Russian newlyweds traditionally went away for a whole month had Jack conceded that ten days in Prague wasn't excessive. Why hadn't he corrected her? Come to think of it, why had he agreed to miss ten days of work? It was as if he had known she would be going off alone.

But that was impossible.

Yegor grunted. "You think the average Ivan and Irina can skip off on a month's vacation? In America, maybe." His eyes twinkled. "In America, I guess you can take a honeymoon whenever you like—married, single, divorced—"

"That's enough!" Lena barked.

"Funny," Rachel said, scraping back her chair, rising to her feet. "So funny, my life."

"Sorry, sorry." Yegor waved his knife, gesturing at her to sit down. "I'll behave, I promise. Sit, sit!"

Across the room, a gray-haired woman wearing a metal neck brace tilted a teacup against her lip, her hand trembling. Rachel took her seat. She would rather be with anyone this morning, even Yegor, than waiting alone for Jack.

Over breakfast—yogurt and a croissant served by matrons who pushed themselves off from the bar like languid swimmers when summoned—Yegor told Rachel about the excursion he had planned for the three of them: a trip to a church outside the city. A chapel filled with old bones, Lena explained, and made a face.

"Not just old bones," Yegor said. "Victims of the plague. Not the most romantic honeymoon destination, Rachel, but I think you'll enjoy it."

The promise of Jack watching her enter the lobby with her new friends at the end of a long day of sight-seeing, Rachel decided, might just barely outweigh the irritation of a day in Yegor's presence.

His interview at the American embassy had gone well, Yegor told Rachel as the train pulled slowly out of Prague, past the gray backs of buildings. Rachel sat across from the couple in the four-person compartment; Lena was knitting a baby blanket with yellow and green yarn. "But I thought the one in Moscow went well, too," he added. "It's all just a popularity contest, I guess." He looked at Rachel as if waiting for her to explain her country's political caprices; when she didn't, he kept on talking. It would be a day or two before he received news. "That reminds me." He rooted through his wallet. "How old are your parents, Rachel?"

"Um . . . father, fifty-eight, mother, fifty-six."

He unfolded a newspaper clipping and handed it to her. It was a graph, the line sloping gradually from the top left to the lower right. Yegor moved next to her and traced the legend with his index finger. " 'Life Expectancy of Russian Men,' " he read. " 'Average age of death.' " He pointed at a dot on the line marked "63.5." "That's the first year of the decline, 1991." His fingertip followed the descending line. "Fifty-seven—that's last year's figure." The line become perforated and careened down-ward. The last year on the graph, 2048, was marked "50." "That's the future."

"The future," Rachel echoed.

"A Russian boy born this year will live to be fifty years old."

Rachel shook her head. She knew it was bad, but fifty? "What's going on?"

"Heart disease, alcoholism, drug abuse . . ." Yegor looked at Lena.

"Murder, pollution, suicide . . ." Lena clicked off the words with her knitting needles.

"Stress," Yegor said. "And not just for men. For women!"

"Stress." Rachel touched her neck. "Sometimes, in Mos-cow, at night, it's hard for me to breathe."

"*Astma!*" Yegor shouted.

"Yes!" Rachel cried. "Asthma!" Once, Rachel had overheard Jack consulting their friend Polina, a medical student, about the nights she woke up, unable to catch anything but the shallowest of breaths. "*Stress*, probably," Polina said. "*Panika. Nervi.*" Sitting up in bed during her next attack, Rachel wheezed, "It's not stress. It's not panic. It's not nerves. It's exhaust fumes from the Garden Ring Road." Jack rubbed her back but wouldn't admit she was right.

"Meanwhile," Yegor said, "everyone close to you, Rachel, will have a long, healthy life."

"That's not true." She was used to correcting such audacities. No, not every American woman has a fur coat. Yes, we get depressed, too, millions of us! "Who's safe?" she said to Yegor. "Can be sickness, how to say, death from car—"

"But don't you see, Rachel?" He waved the graph in the air. "You have better *odds*. Your line goes up; ours goes down."

Lena looked up from her knitting. "Rachel's right. You can't predict what will happen. You have to have trust."

"I don't need trust," Yegor muttered. "I need an American visa."

In Sedlec, the cab let them out at the end of a dead-end street. Beyond a high stone wall stood a small church, its twin, stumpy spires topped with hammered-metal skulls and crossbones. Lena settled on a bench with her knitting. Rachel wanted to stay outside, too; she had a mild headache from the stuffy train, and she felt awkward going off with Yegor. But he was already ushering her ahead, through the cemetery and the church's massive wooden doors. In the dim foyer, he bought their tickets. English was printed beneath the Czech:

YOU ARE ENTERING A PIOUS SPACE. CONSERVE, PLEASE, RESPEKT TO THE DEAD.

At the bottom of the Ossuary's broad flight of steps, cages were cut into the walls, each stacked high with bones, arm and leg nubs neatly interlocked. Garlands of skulls draped from the corners of the ceiling to the center, meeting at an intricate chandelier made of jawbones forced open like animal traps. Miniature obelisks displayed skulls; candleholders were bored into craniums. Some tourist girl had left behind a waxy orange kiss on a forehead.

An old woman, white hair piled in a high bun, strolled arm in arm with an elderly gentleman; they paused to peer at each display with mild, polite interest. Across the room, a teenage boy and girl, both in bell-bottoms that grazed the floor, hung mutely on each other. Rachel joined Yegor in front of one of the bone-heap cages, the wire fencing decorated with a coat of arms made of leg bones and spines.

"Just think." Yegor was enraptured. "These bones lay around for five hundred years before someone decided to make something beautiful out of them."

"Beautiful?" Human remains turned into morbid kitsch by a Czech woodcutter? "It's . . ." She had no idea how to say "grotesque" in Russian.

"It's profound," Yegor nodded. "A place like this, it makes you think about your place in the world, eh?" His voice rumbled next to Rachel's ear. "If I don't get the visa, Lena's not going to America by herself to give birth." He glanced at her. "Of course, if there were someone I trusted to be with her in my place, a friend who could help her . . ."

The chapel's unrelenting grays and whites had filtered the color from his face. Rachel felt her own cheeks drain until they were as cool as the stone wall she braced herself against.

"I'd like to make a proposal, Rachel," Yegor continued, "based on the possibility that you might return to America soon. You could look after Lena. Find her a place to stay, a nice hotel in Chicago, if you like—though I'd prefer a warmer climate, somewhere with less heavy industry—and a hospital, a doctor. Translate for her, help her through the birth, look after them until they're ready to come home."

Rachel shook her head, pretending not to understand, shaken not only by his request but by the way it made her heart pound.

"Money's not an issue," Yegor said, his gaze steady. No one, she thought—not Jack or his friends or her tutor—had ever put so much faith in her comprehension of the Russian language. "I'll pay you whatever's fair, and cover all of the expenses."

"Yegor, it's not the money. I just don't—"

"It's true we haven't known each other very long, Rachel, but—"

"Two days! Does Lena know about this?"

He looked away. "She didn't want me to ask."

"You need an American. That's why . . ." That's why they helped her into town. That's why Lena took her arm during their stroll.

"I know some Americans in Moscow," he said. "I wouldn't trust my cat with them. But it's true: I had a feeling when I saw you at the airport helping Lena with the stupid suitcase. I knew we could trust you."

In the lower corner of the family crest, a bone-bird perched on a shoulder bone, pecking at a skull's eye socket with a long, sharp beak. "Yegor," Rachel said, "Jack is coming here. Today, probably."

"Jack."

"My boyfriend."

"Your fiancé," Yegor corrected.

"Yes, of course."

"You're happy together in Moscow." Yegor's expression was hungry and bold; Rachel had seen the look before. When she took the GRE, in an auditorium in Moscow, a small group of Russians near her whispered and passed notes throughout the test. During the analogies, the sallow, greasy-haired young man next to her began glancing at her answer sheet. Their passports were out on the counter for identification—his red, hers blue. She put hers in her back pocket, shielded her answer sheet with her elbow, and glared at him. He stared back.

Good fortune was wasted on her, the look said.

"I don't understand," Rachel said. "Why so important, to go to America?"

Yegor rubbed his eyes and turned away. "Do you know the word *vikidish*?"

She shook her head.

"It's when a baby dies before it's born. This happened to Lena. To us. Twice."

"I'm sorry." She touched his arm, but he wouldn't look at her. "I didn't know."

He pulled away and headed for the staircase. "I tell you not for pity, but only so you'll understand."

She followed after him. "I want to help, but I can't. It's impossible."

He nodded without looking back at her.

She was a hypocrite, she told herself as they trudged up the steps and pushed into the glaring gray light. She was as pessimistic about Russia as Yegor—it was Jack who was naïve—but she wouldn't help them, not if it meant risking her future with Jack.

Outside, Lena was gone from her bench. Yegor headed down the street, breaking into a run. "Check the cemetery," he called over his shoulder.

Rachel circled the church. Plants rotted on the stone slabs. Black-and-white photos were shellacked to some of the graves: a young woman with bobbed hair in a dotted-swiss dress; a stern man, also young, in glasses with thick black frames. Birds twittered frantically in a high tree. No sign of Lena.

Out on the street, Rachel found them embracing. Lena

held an ice-cream cone at arm's length, the pink scoop threatening to topple. Rachel hung back, but she couldn't shut out Yegor's quavering tones of fear and reproach.

"*Ne ischezai. Nikodga ne ischezai,*" he begged his wife. "Don't disappear. Don't ever disappear again."

Back at the hotel, there was no sign of Jack, no messages at the desk. Rachel turned down Lena's offer to join them for dinner and headed up to her room.

That night she read, skimming gossipy encounters with Bunin, Bely, Nabokov, slowing down as Berberova described Khodasevich's illness, his lethargy, and above all his heartbreak at losing Russia. Exhausted, Berberova found herself hardening against him. Rachel had assumed the couple spent their life together, but no. She wondered if they had even been married.

> In 1932, when I finally left our Billancourt apartment, a not too malicious wit recounted the circumstances:
>
> "She cooked him enough borshch for three days, darned all the socks, and then left."
>
> This was almost the truth.

Rachel turned off the light, hugged her pillow, and let herself think about what it would be like to take care of Lena in Chicago. Her parents might be willing to give up their guest room to a pregnant stranger, if it meant Rachel would be safely back at home. She and her mother could take Lena to Lamaze class and help her through the birth—Rachel would be too scared to do it on her own. She imagined her father driving them all to the hospital in the middle of the night. They would have to get a crib until Lena and the baby were strong enough to travel. Then what? Rachel would fly with them, of course. Back to Moscow, and to Jack. Because if she didn't—if she

waited instead for him to come home—she might never see
him again.

He called in the middle of the night, shouting above laughter and a disco beat. His friends were throwing him a party at
the apartment in case he didn't come back. There had been
some problems today, an accident on the metro, the highways
jammed, but he was leaving for the airport in a few hours.

When the phone rang again, as Rachel was heading out for
breakfast, she almost didn't answer it. Maybe that would keep
the bad news at bay.

It was Jack's friend Zhenya, calling from Moscow. While he
asked her in English about the weather, the bridge, the castle, she
looked out the window at another piercing gray sky, waiting.

"Rachel, there is a problem," Zhenya said finally. "Jack is
sick. He says to tell you he has the gives. No, not gives. Hives."

"Hives? Jack has hives?"

"Yeh, hives." Zhenya snickered. He was the most solemn
person she had ever met, but at certain moments it became ap-
parent there was no aspect of life he took seriously. He was a
Dostoevsky scholar. "He is sleeping now, very tired from medicine. So, will he come to Praga? It's an interesting question."
He sighed. "We hope for best, Rachel, but the things become
as always they do."

She walked to Lena and Yegor's room, her feelings just beyond her grasp, like soap bubbles she was chasing down the
hall. Jack had told her about the severe attacks of hives that he
used to have as a boy each year before school began. Anxiety,
his doctor diagnosed; nothing to do but ride it out. He'd spend
a week in bed, doped up on allergy medicine as the welts crept
slowly down his body. The attacks stopped in college. He had-
n't had one since.

Lena, in the pink bathrobe that Rachel had folded at the

airport, wet hair combed back, ushered Rachel into the room. A pair of twin beds was pushed together in the middle of the room, the sheets tangled. Yegor was shaving at the sink, shirtless, wet hair swirling on his flabby chest. "What's the matter?" he said, wiping his face on a towel. Lena pulled up a chair for Rachel.

"It's psychological," Rachel concluded after telling them about Zhenya's call.

Lena nodded. "Stress."

"He doesn't want to leave Moscow," Rachel said. "He thinks they won't give him another Russian visa."

"Ha!" Yegor snorted at her from the sink. "Our country has bigger problems than lazy tourists, Rachel."

"Jack's not a tourist."

"What is he, then, a Russian? I'll tell you something, Rachel. A Russian man would never send his wife off on her honeymoon alone."

Rachel stood up. "I'm not his wife," she said. "We're not married."

"Exactly! What's stopping you?"

"It's none of your business!"

He waved his razor in the air. "Maybe not, but Lena and I can't help wondering: Why doesn't Rachel's Jack want to come to Prague? Why won't he marry her?"

"That's enough," Lena said.

Yegor crossed his beefy arms over his chest. "Most of all, we ask ourselves, why would Rachel want to marry such a selfish, irresponsible person?"

"You don't know him!" Rachel said.

"What about you? Do you know him?"

"No!" Rachel shouted, and then, "I mean, that's enough!"

Lena followed Rachel out the door and back to her room, apologizing with each step. "He's nervous. It's got nothing to do with you."

"He's mad at me," Rachel said. "Because I won't take you to America." Lena shook her head no, no, but Rachel eased the door closed.

The Russian embassy in Prague stood at the top of an incline. The building was modern, pieced together from white blocks streaked with grime. Rachel paused at the gate to catch her breath. She had taken a tram to the castle and moved at a fast clip through this quiet neighborhood of embassies—Syria, Albania, Belgium, Kuwait—where glum-faced guards paced behind wrought-iron fences. Past the Russian embassy's glass front doors, silhouettes moved beneath a thin beam of light. Inside it would be stuffy and crowded, filled with Russians pushing, asking questions in querulous tones.

Rachel sat down on the embassy's low stone wall. Cars rumbled fast up the brick hill and vanished over the slope. She unbuttoned her coat and swiped at her sweaty neck. In Moscow it was the dead of winter. She thought of her daily commute. She saw a woman pulling a staggering man across the icy square in front of the metro. By the entrance, an old kerchiefed woman hunched over her outstretched palm, muttering and crossing herself again and again. On the train a man rested his chapped hands on his knees, his black-rimmed fingernails like ancient coins just unearthed. Rachel ached to be there, but just thinking of it exhausted her. Jack's friends would have to take care of him; maybe he could still join her for the tail end of the trip. With him or without him, she would renew her visa another day. She could not make herself walk through the embassy's front door.

She returned to the riverbank and wandered the curving streets beneath the castle. In a walled park she read about Berberova, who was building a new life in Paris, alone:

The Palais des Invalides was visible from my window, and on the other side the Eiffel Tower lights flashed at night. The room was on the sixth floor, and you had to climb a narrow, steep staircase; the window opened out of a sloping ceiling; behind the screen, where there was a wash basin, stood a spirit lamp on which I could brew myself tea, so that I needn't always dine on cold food.

When she heard the knock, Rachel opened her door a crack. A bouquet of pink roses muscled into the room. Jack!

But it was Yegor, his stubbled head dewy, polo shirt clinging to his chest in wet patches; his soapy smell overpowered the roses' scent. Lena stood on tiptoes behind him. He didn't get his visa, Rachel thought. They were courting her again. This time she might listen.

"There's a card," Yegor said.

"Dearest Rachel!" it read. "Deepest apologies, Yegor."

They wanted to take her out for supper, her choice. The Czech food she'd sampled was like German cuisine ruined by Soviet chefs—sausages and dumplings bloating in pools of oil—so Rachel picked a Chinese restaurant that glowed like a lantern at the intersection of two Old Town alleys. Inside, oblivious to the rumpled clusters of tourists, Czech couples held hands across tabletops. On the thick menus, English translations were printed beneath the Czech. Lena nodded politely at Rachel's broken-Russian descriptions of Chinese dishes.

"Congratulate me, Rachel," Yegor said after their drinks had come. He cracked apart his chopsticks and rubbed them together furiously, as if hoping for sparks. "Today I was granted an American visa."

She felt them watching her intently. "Congratulations." She raised her beer, forcing a smile. "You'll have an American baby after all."

"American-born, but Russian-bred," Yegor said as their glasses clinked.

They were returning to Moscow the next day, and they wanted Rachel to fly back with them. She hadn't renewed her visa yet, she explained. She thought of the Russian embassy, the moldering concrete block on the hill. When would she ever have the strength to go back there?

"We don't like to think of you here all alone," Lena said.

"But I have to finish my *myedovii myesyats*," Rachel said.

Yegor let out a guffaw that provoked scowls from the young lovers at the next table. The waiter arrived, uncovering an enormous tin pot of rice with a flourish, filling the space above the table with a cloud of steam. Rachel watched as Lena's face emerged from the veil, then Yegor's, twin moons rising from fog.

The next afternoon, Rachel took a final walk with Lena along the bank of the Vltava. Three little girls tossed scraps of bread into the wind; white gulls swooped to catch them. Leaning against the railing with Lena, facing the castle, Rachel thought of Berberova, alone at her window in Paris. "Maybe I'll go to the opera tonight," she said.

"I wish I could go with you." Lena smiled. "Yegor hates the opera."

They exchanged business cards, and Rachel jotted down her parents' phone number in Chicago, though Yegor had set his sights on Miami.

"I think I . . . wish I were going with you," Rachel said. "To America."

Lena cradled her stomach against the cold. "You can if you want to."

"But I don't have a reason." The wind had picked up, and

Rachel began to shiver. Overhead, in the distance, she heard a mechanical flapping, growing louder. "No reason at all."

"Of course you do," Lena said, seeking and holding Rachel's gaze. "It might not be me, or Yegor. It might not even be Jack."

Rachel didn't dare breathe, let alone speak.

"Don't you know what it is, Rachel?"

Something dark swung into a high corner of the sky. The flapping echoed loudly behind them.

Down the bank, a helicopter hovered above a building, towing something from a cable. An enormous geodesic dome made of steel spikes and glass.

"Look!" Lena cried. "Do you remember what that building is?"

"Yes!" Rachel shouted above the racket. Lena had pointed it out to her on their first day in Prague: the Ginger and Fred Building. Two famous architects, one American, one Czech, had designed it together. The building looked like a pair of dancers—two curvy tubes whirling around a corner. The man stood proud and tall, chest jutting, windows popping like buttons. The woman's wide glass skirt rose gracefully from the ground, cinching at the waist as she swooned against her partner.

The dome swayed on its cable. Slowly, the helicopter began to lower its cargo.

"He's getting a hat!" Lena shouted as the wind dashed against them from the river.

The dome settled gently onto its moorings. The helicopter rose slightly, and the end of the cable swished free, bouncing wildly through the air. Rachel cried out, ecstatic with fear, watching the future unfurl before her, as vast as the white sky.

ACKNOWLEDGMENTS

I am so grateful to my family and friends for their support and encouragement during the writing of this book. For their boundless kindness and patience, I thank Marguerite Delacoma and Robert Shonk, my parents; my brother, Bob, and my sister, Carrie; Wynne Delacoma; and Molly Anderson and Elizabeth Ward.

Teachers, classmates, editors, friends, and family members offered comments that improved the stories and spurred me forward. I am grateful to all, especially those who took on draft after draft without complaint: Michael Adams, Janice Deal, Elizabeth Harris, Junse Kim, Marylee MacDonald, and Susan Miller.

I am grateful to Ethan Nosowsky, my editor, for his advocacy and his discoveries. Many thanks to Amy Williams, my ingenious and enthusiastic agent. I am indebted to Max Bazerman, boss and friend, for his confidence in me. I thank Fred Shafer for helping me finish and, even more, for guiding me through the many stories that preceded these.